THE BOARD OF THE EARTH

He turns to stare at me and I wonder how that is possible. This is a dream. A dream of long ago. Emrys should be long dead.

"Who are you?" I say. "How can you see me?"

"I am the *Emrys," he says. "And though death came for me long ago, I see you now through the power of magics I cast long before you were born."*

"I don't understand," I say.

"That much, at least, is clear," he says. "Come." He strides to the center of the field and I follow, a mere shadow to his reality in this dream.

We reach the altar, and Emrys removes the wooden object from it, and then connects it to the Board of the Earth. It is obviously not *a Board itself, but somehow it . . .*

"Ties them together," he says, looking up. "When you have all the Boards assembled, this piece is the one that will unite them and give you the power of elemental binding."

"What is *the power of elemental binding?"*

"The power to use the four primary elements of this world together, and the fifth element that binds them all." He smiles at me and adds, "Many of the difficulties that plague you now will be relieved once you have all the Boards and the key in your possession."

Elated, I ask, "Where is the Board of the Earth?"

"All will be made clear to you . . . in due time."

Keeper of the Winds
Keeper of the Waters
Keeper of the Flames
Keeper of the Earth

Keeper of the Earth

DAUGHTER OF DESTINY

JENNA SOLITAIRE

TOR

A TOM DOHERTY ASSOCIATES BOOK
NEW YORK

KEEPER OF THE EARTH

A Tor Teen Book
Published by Tom Doherty Associates, LLC
175 Fifth Avenue
New York, NY 10010

www.tor.com

Library of Congress Cataloging-in-Publication Data

Solitaire, Jenna.
Keeper of the earth / Jenna Solitaire.
p. cm.—(Daughter of destiny)
Summary: After finding the Board of Fire, Jenna and Simon must decipher the clues that will lead them to the Board of Earth before they come face-to-face with a relentless enemy who has coveted the Boards for millennia.
ISBN-13: 978-0-765-35360-3
ISBN-10: 0-765-35360-1
[1. Supernatural—Fiction. 2. Adventure and adventurers—Fiction. 3. Magic—Fiction. 4. Vatican City—Fiction.] I. Title.

PZ7.S6892Ker 2006
[Fic]—dc22

First Tor Teen Edition: October 2006

Printed in the United States of America

0 9 8 7 6 5 4 3 2 1

For my mother, who once paid for me to take a journey to a distant place . . . in pennies.

Keeper of the Earth

DAUGHTER OF DESTINY

PROLOGUE

I open my eyes to a large field surrounded by stunted evergreens. The trees look out of place, as though they're trying to grow in hostile dirt. The grass before me is the dark, rich green of perfect-cut emeralds. Dew sparkles on each blade, a diamond complement. Hills undulate in the distance and from here I see that these trees are a rarity—they are either dying or being cut down. Soon, there will be nothing here but the rocks, the hills and the emerald grass.

Standing in the shadowy cover of pine boughs, I watch as two figures meet in the field. Both move with the careful dignity of age and station, their robes flowing around them like brown and gray waves. Each holds a large wooden staff—one as though it's a part of his hand, and the other as though it is a treasure. A large stone sits like an altar between them, holding an oddly shaped piece of wood scored with hundreds of tiny runes. It looks like a star, but lopsided. It is magnified in my eyes.

The two men speak, the tone of their words harsh.

"You would die for this . . . bauble, Emrys?" With a disdainful gesture, the man on the left, the one

who holds his staff so tightly that his knuckles are white, points at the wooden object on the altar.

"A thousand times if I must. Seek power elsewhere, Coghlan. This power is not for mortal hands."

"You are mortal, Emrys. Accept my challenge and I will prove it to you."

The man called Emrys sighs, and I see how sad he looks, like a man who already knows what is about to happen. "I am many things, Coghlan, but not mortal as you understand the term. Will you not cease in your hunt?"

"Never. The powers of the Board and of elemental binding must be mine. I will not rest until both are in my grasp."

"Then I accept your challenge," Emrys says. "I am sorry for you."

"Save your pity, Emrys," Coghlan says. "I need it not."

The two men walk away from each other, following rules they both know and that I cannot fathom.

As Emrys turns, a ball of fire roars through the air toward his head, a spinning orb that grows larger as it moves. He raises his right hand and the fireball hits an invisible field, ricocheting into a nearby group of stones and bursting into a million sparks of red, yellow and orange.

Two nearby trees groan as Coghlan mutters incantations and gestures with his staff. He tears them from the ground by their roots, and hurls them through the air with terrific force.

Emrys raises his hand again, and the invisible

shield deflects the huge missiles, sending them crashing to the ground in a spray of earth and broken branches. Emrys then gestures toward the sky and overhead, I see a swirling cloud of fire begin to form.

Beads of sweat stand on Coghlan's brow as he hurries to prepare another assault. Emrys waits, his face bearing the same sad expression.

With a shout, Coghlan points a finger and it seems that every stone in the field flies into the air, arcing toward his enemy. A thousand missiles, each one capable of striking a fatal blow, hurtle toward Emrys.

And each one slams into the invisible shield, clattering to the ground in knee-high piles of rocks that look like burial mounds.

"Your powers are not strong enough to challenge mine," Emrys calls. "You will leave me no choice but to destroy you." Above, the clouds have taken on the fiery form of a large bird that is both beautiful and terrible to behold. Its wings blaze in violet and red flames, its body the glowing embers of a star. The bird cries once, the sound echoing over the field. I flinch in reaction—its call is at once mournful and disturbing.

This is the legendary phoenix, I think. It spreads its wings to their full majesty for a moment, a beacon of fire, then tucks them in and dives.

"The powers of the Boards must be mine!" At the last second, Coghlan looks up and sees the phoenix hurtling toward him. He reaches into his robe and removes a long, wooden wand. "You were never so

weak as to need a familiar, Emrys!" he cries, pointing it at the creature.

A thin beam of silver light shoots from the tip of the wand and slams into the phoenix. An explosion of sparks burns in the sky and the wounded bird furls its wings, crumpling to the earth.

Emrys reaches into his own robes and removes a Board. This one is shaped much the same as the others that are already in my possession, though the distance is too great for me to make out the runes that undoubtedly score the surface of the Board. Emrys points a long, thin finger, and it is then that I realize he is old. Old beyond counting for a human. And so very tired.

In the center of the field, a cube of stone flies into the air, glowing runes appearing on its side as it rises. The falling phoenix and rising stone collide, and another brilliant shower of sparks bursts in the air. Then the phoenix is gone and the stone falls to the ground. The runes on its side flicker crimson for a moment, and then fade.

"He is not *my familiar, Coghlan," Emrys says. "He is one of my guardians. A benefit I am granted for my protection of the Board of the Earth and the key to elemental binding." He points once more and calls out in a voice deeper and more resonant with power than before. "Leave, Coghlan, lest I call upon my true abilities and destroy you."*

"Never!" Coghlan screams. He points his wand at Emrys and the silvery beam flashes again.

It strikes the shield and dissipates harmlessly.

"Enough, then," Emrys says. He makes an almost negligent gesture, his eyes sad and weary.

The ground rumbles around us, and Coghlan's eyes widen. He tries to hurry his casting, but the incantation tumbles from his lips in gibbered words, the power he wields untapped in his panic.

Emrys closes his hand into a fist, and beneath Coghlan's feet there is a horrendous sound, like a gigantic sheet being torn asunder. The ground opens under him like a gaping mouth and he falls into the hole, which slams shut behind him. His final, defiant words echo in the air where he stood just a second ago.

"Goodbye, Coghlan," Emrys says. "You poor, pitiful fool."

Then he turns to stare at me and I wonder how that is possible. This is a dream. A dream of long ago. Emrys should be long dead.

"Ah, but what is death," he says, as though reading my thoughts, "to a wizard?"

"I don't know," I admit.

"To most of us, time and death are absolutes—much as they are for normal mortals. To those such as myself and your enemy Malkander, they are merely avoidable truths."

"Who are you?" I say. "How can you see me?"

"I am the *Emrys," he says. "And though death came for me long ago, I see you now through the power of magics I cast long before you were born."*

"Then how . . . ?"

"I possess the Board of the Earth, and the power

of elemental binding," he says. "What is time to me?"

"I don't understand," I say.

"That much, at least, is clear," he says. "Come." He strides to the center of the field and I follow, a mere shadow to his reality in this dream.

We reach the altar, and Emrys removes the wooden object from it, and then connects it to the Board of the Earth. It is obviously not *a Board itself, but somehow it . . .*

"Ties them together," he says, looking up. "When you have all the Boards assembled, this piece is the one that will unite them and give you the power of elemental binding."

"What is *the power of elemental binding?"*

"The power to use the four primary elements of this world together, and the fifth element that binds them all." He smiles at me and adds, "Many of the difficulties that plague you now will be relieved once you have all the Boards and the key in your possession."

Elated, I ask, "Where is the Board of the Earth?"

"All will be made clear to you . . . in due time," he says. "But first, there is a task you must perform for me."

"Task?" I ask.

He picks up the small, rune-marked stone cube where the fiery bird disappeared. "The creature you saw—the phoenix—is both spirit and reality. A guardian of sorts for those who hold the Board of the Earth and the key. This stone is a phylactery—while the phoenix resides inside, no harm can come to his essence. The damage done by Coghlan will have long since healed by your time."

"And?" I ask.

"You must find the stone and bring it to my tomb."

"So where is it?"

"In your long and long ago past, the stone was taken . . ." Emrys stops and shakes his head. Under his breath, I hear him mutter a foul word and something else about the transient nature of time. Then he continues, "The people called the Picts took the stone and placed it atop another as a marker on a battlefield—this field, in fact. You must find the field in your time, locate the marker, and bring the phoenix stone to my place of burial. Only then will I reveal the location of the Board of the Earth and the key piece. Only then will you be ready to accept the mantle of Keeper of the Elements."

With that, he turns and walks across the field, disappearing into the shadows on the far side.

The ground where Coghlan disappeared is unmarked, and then I know for certain this is a dream.

"Wait!" I cry. If the four Boards of the Elements require something else to tie them together, there must be more information I need. "What is the fifth element?" I think a moment, and add, "And where is your tomb?"

His voice comes from nowhere and everywhere. "You have already been given the answer to your first question, Keeper of the Boards. Think on it, and it will come to you in time. As for the location of my tomb, that too, will be made clear to you—when you have the phoenix stone."

I am alone in the field and I look at the altar. The oddly shaped piece of wood is gone. The Board of the Earth is gone. The phoenix stone and the man called Emrys are gone. But this place, this landscape will be here when I awake. Somewhere in Scotland, if Shalizander had not lied. I must memorize it all as best as I can.

All around me the field is silent and waiting, like the land itself is holding its breath, waiting for the turn of the season or the coming of the next age. Or the death of the trees.

It is as though the land knows what is coming and is afraid.

"As expected, young Jenna Solitaire arrived in Rome last night, along with Father Monk. They have taken lodgings near the Vatican."

"You will be meeting her, of course?"

"Yes, along with the others. It is an opportunity I wouldn't miss, if what you have told me is true."

"To lie would serve no purpose in our arrangement. Watch all of them with care. One never knows when someone will let something important slip."

"You must wake up!"

My eyes snapped open at the same time as the voice of the Board of the Flames roared in my mind, banishing the vision created and somehow sent to me by the man called Emrys. Above me, the water-stained ceiling of my room in the Hotel Amalia came into focus.

"What?" I asked with a sigh. *"What is it?"*

"Shalizander speaks, and you must heed her,

Keeper. The time has come." The voice of the Board of the Flames is the crackle and pop of a forest fire.

"My brother speaks the truth," the Board of the Waters added in its smoothest voice, the one I had come to associate with a babbling brook. *"The ritual of the dagger must be performed,"* it continued. *"The power of Shalizander is not to be denied."*

"Yes," the Board of the Winds hissed in the voice of a high wind. *"Power is your destiny."*

"Shut up!" My eyes felt grainy and raw, my throat was sore from a long night of little sleep and disturbing dreams. Not even the words of power I'd learned from Dario in Pompeii seemed to help for very long. Between the Boards and Shalizander, the haunting dreams and visions, I hadn't slept well in days.

"Daughter, let me help you," Shalizander said, my ultimate ancestor, now another voice in my head, entering the fray. *"Once you have completed the ritual—"*

"I'll be under your control," I snapped. *"No thanks!"*

The Boards and Shalizander were blessedly quiet for a moment, and I took advantage of the silence to think about what I had learned from the vision of the wizard named Emrys. It seemed clear that in order to get to the fourth Board—the Board of the Earth—I would have to follow his directions. But who he was and if he could be trusted were questions I had no answers to at the moment.

Glancing at my watch, I saw that it was only a

few minutes after four in the morning. Simon and I had arrived in Rome late the night before and I was still tired. It seemed like I was always tired now—tired of traveling, tired of fighting, and tired of listening to the Boards and Shalizander constantly clamoring in my mind.

All they seemed to want now was for me to complete the ritual of the dagger, giving Shalizander access to my mind and body, but gaining her magical powers in return.

I stretched, and as the Board of the Winds began to speak, I muttered, *"Vixisthra!"* commanding it to fall silent again. I didn't know how long it would last, and tried to fall back asleep. Since becoming the Keeper of the Boards, I'd learned that even sleep filled with dreams and visions and voices was better than no sleep at all.

Usually.

But I drifted into memory, and that was sometimes as bad as any vision or dream I'd ever had.

. . . Early spring, and the rain falls in a light drizzle. My grandfather is dead, and I stand at his funeral. A college student, nineteen and adrift. The last of my family is gone. Father Andrew speaks Catholic words of comfort. Nearby, a man with dark hair and dark eyes watches. . . .

. . . The wind howls outside the attic of my grandfather's house as I pick up a strange-looking board hidden in my grandmother's keepsake trunk. It reminds me a little of a Ouija board. I place my hands on the planchette and call out for my mother,

my grandmother—anyone. The wind answers with the name "Shalizander" . . . .

. . . Flashes of Simon in my hometown of Miller's Crossing, Ohio. Standing on my front step with Father Andrew. Helping me out of the river. Sharing with me the truth of my destiny. Fighting side-by-side with the Templar Knight Armand and his men as I lost control of the Board of the Winds and it called tornadoes to ravage the entire city. Simon saving me from the Board and from myself . . .

My best friend, Tom Anderson, injured and paralyzed and blessedly alive. Kristen Evers's love for him, and both of them telling me goodbye. Reminding me that my quest to find all the Boards is necessary for the whole world and I can't be selfish about it . . .

. . . Visiting Jerusalem and meeting Saduj Nomed. His amber eyes burn into mine. I feel loved and safe. Searching the desert for the Board of the Waters. Finding the Board in Petra, the City of the Dead. Learning that what I thought had happened between Saduj and myself didn't. It was all part of his illusion as an incubus. Realizing what I truly felt for Simon, and that he could never be mine . . .

. . . Making our way to Naples. Hearing the howls of the stray dogs and having one of them befriend me as a guardian while I was there. Meeting Dario—the man who turned out to be my great-grandfather—and learning my first words in the Language of the Birds, my first attempts at truly

controlling the Boards, instead of them controlling me . . .

. . . Climbing up the side of Mount Vesuvius and watching the man I thought was Simon kill Dario, only to figure out too late that it was his twin brother, Peraud. Inside the volcano, the air sulfur-filled and scorching, wrangling with the Board of the Flames and eventually mastering it. Choosing to fight Peraud, to destroy him once and for all. Finding Shalizander's dagger and believing that Peraud was dead and Simon was safe . . .

. . . Realizing that Shalizander, my ultimate grandmother and one of the people who had created the Boards, wasn't really dead, but somehow had used her magic and the dagger to preserve her spirit in a magical realm. That she wanted me to perform the ritual that would give her access to my body and mind, and me access to her powers . . .

"Yes, my daughter, take the dagger and perform the ritual. You must if you are to defeat Malkander, and truly become the Daughter of Destiny."

. . . Malkander, Shalizander's lover and also one of the creators. Peraud's master. Simon's father. An evil shadow whose magic has preserved his life all these years as he's attempted to gain control over the Boards and fulfill his own prophecy . . .

"The dagger, daughter! You must use the dagger!"

"Listen to Shalizander, Keeper. She speaks the truth!"

. . . Understanding that the ritual would cost me

more than just sharing my body, but possibly my very soul. My identity . . .

"It need not be that way, daughter. Malizander was always stubborn. She fought when we could have been two powerful allies in the same body. The way of the dagger is the only way! Your control over the Boards is tenuous, daughter! Don't you understand? My strength will be your strength!"

. . . Someone knocking at the door, always someone bothering me, demanding more than I want to give. Always the voices of the Boards, inside my mind like memories that won't fade away. And now her voice, Shalizander's voice. Demanding, begging, insisting . . .

"Take it in your hand and strike! The magic will keep you safe."

. . . Knocking at the door . . .

"Do it! Strike now, before it's too late!"

My eyes snapped open, and I saw the dagger clenched in my right fist, set to plunge into my heart. A simple ritual that would let Shalizander escape the magical world she'd created for herself and into this one . . . through me.

I felt the muscles in my arm tighten, my lungs squeeze tight. The shining blade was inches away from my chest and I could feel my arms trembling with the strain of the conflicting messages.

"No," I said. *"It is* my *choice!"*

Someone knocked on the door again, and I heard Simon's voice. "Jenna? Are you all right?"

I couldn't trust myself anymore. Even in my sleep,

the Boards and Shalizander could still force me to complete the ritual. And that was something I just couldn't bring myself to do. Not yet, and not unless there was no other choice.

"What makes you think there are other choices, daughter?" Shalizander's voice hissed in my mind. *"You cannot—"*

"No!"

"Daughter—"

"No!" I shouted aloud, throwing the dagger across the room. I heard the clatter of it hitting the floor and then sliding beneath the rickety dresser where my meager set of clothing was stored. "You don't own me!"

"And you never will," I added. *"Not even to save the world."*

"Jenna!" Simon called again, pounding on the door even harder. "What's wrong?"

"Yes!" I knew that if I didn't answer him quickly, he'd break down the door. "What is it?"

"Are you all right?" he called. "I heard you shouting."

"I was sleeping. Dreaming."

"May I come in?" he asked.

Realizing that I was still flat on my back and my whole body was still shaking, I said, "Just a minute."

I got up and made my way across the room, taking deep breaths to steady myself before I unlocked the door. Opening it, I found Simon on the other side, wearing his freshly laundered clergyman clothes, complete with the white collar and black suitcoat. His dark hair had been neatly trimmed and styled, and his blue eyes bored into my green ones as though he could see every secret of my soul. "Everything all right?" he asked.

"Fine," I said. "I was just trying to get some rest. The dreams got the better of me. Again."

He looked past me into the room. "I know you could use the extra sleep." His voice was smooth and deep and calming. "But you haven't had much luck with that recently."

"Do I ever?" I snapped, and then sighed. "I'm sorry, Simon. I'm more tired than I thought."

"Understandable, given everything you've been through." He gave my rumpled clothing the once-over. "You—are going to change before we go to the Vatican, yes?"

"No, I thought my dirty jeans and torn sweat shirt would be just the outfit for greeting your superiors," I said, resuming my deep, calming breaths—for an entirely different reason this time. "Give me some credit, Simon. I know how important it is to you that we make a good impression."

Simon placed a gentle hand on my arm, dissipating my anger with his warm touch.

"I'm sorry," he said. "I just want this to go well. The last thing we need is the powers that be in the Vatican asking too many questions. It would only hinder us—and put needless lives in jeopardy—should they decide to send additional agents with us in search of the Boards."

"I understand," I said. "I'll change before we

leave, and I promise to look like a proper young lady from the Midwest."

Simon smiled. "Well, that might be asking a bit much."

I laughed, unable to help myself. Simon rarely made a joke, but after everything we'd been through together, he had finally begun to loosen up a little. "Besides, if nothing else, I'm looking forward to seeing Father Andrew again."

"That's good to hear," he said. "Perhaps seeing him will lift your spirits. You've been very internally focused since Dario passed."

I didn't say anything, just nodded and crossed to the small dresser where I'd stored my few clothes. Losing Dario hurt more than I wanted to admit. He had been my great-grandmother's lover, and together they had begun exploring the secrets of the Board of the Winds. Though I had only known him for a few days, he had treated me kindly and kept his—and my great-grandmother's—secret, even when it wasn't necessary. Somehow he'd known that my focus had to be on retrieving the Board of the Flames, not on reuniting with a long-lost family member.

I pulled out a clean pair of black jeans and a dark purple blouse to go over my tank top, and tossed them on the bed. "As you can see, my clothing selection is somewhat limited."

"That should be fine," Simon replied. "But you'll need something else. Hold on a moment."

He stepped back to the door and reached into the

hallway, then came back carrying a gift-wrapped box. "For you," he said.

I've always loved getting presents, but the idea of Simon actually going out and buying me something was really amazing. He wasn't much of a shopper.

"Thank you," I said, tearing open the paper. Inside was a black leather coat, perfect for the cool air of Rome in the springtime. "I love it!"

Simon smiled. "I thought you might," he said. "Besides, that denim jacket of yours has seen better days."

I glanced at the battered jacket I'd been dragging with me since we left Miller's Crossing and smiled. "Well, you're right about that anyway," I said, taking the new coat from the box and slipping it on. The leather was buttery soft and the lining of the jacket warm against my skin. "It's perfect."

"I'm glad you like it," he said. "Why don't you get cleaned up and dressed? I'll meet you downstairs and we can have a cup of coffee before we leave."

"All right," I said, "but you're buying."

"I'm just a poor man of the cloth," Simon objected. "I've already spent my life savings on your new coat. You're the one with the hefty bank account."

"I'm trying to teach myself to be frugal and save," I said with a straight face. "Wherever we go from here, I figure we should bicycle instead of fly."

I enjoyed teasing Simon about money, and he hadn't taken it well initially, but he'd slowly gotten into the spirit of things.

"Very funny," he said, "but I'm feeling generous today, so I'll buy."

"Look at that. We've only been in Rome one day and already a miracle!"

Simon laughed. "Do you really like the coat?" he asked. "I thought you might like having something nice and new."

"It's great," I said, meaning it. "I'll wear it today, and not even bring my old one along for comfort's sake."

Shaking his head and still smiling, Simon said, "I'll see you downstairs." Then he stepped out of the room, shutting the door quietly behind him.

Once he was gone, I sat down on the bed. I didn't want Simon to know how much I was struggling with the Boards and Shalizander—not yet, anyway. He had told me that the Vatican was a place of many intrigues, and there were very few people in it that weren't reaching for greater power or attempting to ascend closer to the Pope's inner circle. He would need all his focus, and if he thought I was having new problems, his attention could be diverted at a critical moment.

The sad truth—that I could only admit to myself—was that I was in serious trouble. I couldn't sleep without dreaming—usually dreams of other Keepers or Holders, sometimes dreams of my family, sometimes just nightmares. The Keepers were the women in my direct family line—each of them charged with the legacy of the Board of the Winds, handed down from mother to daughter since the time of Shalizander. The Holders were those who had somehow managed to find a Board and use some of its powers, but were not in the bloodline.

Dreams like that, I could usually handle. Sometimes, they were even instructive. But mostly they were tiring. I don't think anyone should have to dream vividly every night, all night long.

I couldn't concentrate for more than a few minutes at a time, and every time I relaxed the slightest bit, one of the Boards—or more frequently, Shalizander herself—would push me to complete the ritual. All of them were hungry for power, for the prophecy to be fulfilled.

The Boards spoke repeatedly of "opening the way," but had yet to tell me what exactly that meant. From everything I'd been able to piece together from the Chronicle—the journal that had been kept by every Keeper since Shalizander's time—the opening of the way would be a bad thing. Yet it appeared that Shalizander herself now wanted to do whatever that was. Or maybe she believed it was necessary, according to the prophecy—which I had yet to learn. It was all very confusing and so much information came in scattered bits and pieces that understanding it at all seemed impossible.

I quickly showered and changed, happy that for now that the Boards seemed quiet, and excited to be seeing Father Andrew again. He'd been a part of my family for years, and had presided over the funerals of my parents and both my grandparents.

He'd also introduced me to Simon. The man I loved and couldn't have. The man who said he cared for me, but wouldn't let those feelings get in the way of what we had to do. I sighed and tossed my damp towel over the side of the tub, then ran a brush through my hair. What would really be nice was a few days off, some good nights of uninterrupted sleep, maybe a trip to a mall, and a long massage.

I looked at myself in the mirror. My long, red hair needed a trim, and there were dark circles under my eyes. I pulled my hair back into a ponytail and did what I could to hide the circles with the little bit of makeup I had with me. Stepping out of the bathroom, I picked up the battered backpack that contained the three Boards, the Chronicle, and my BlackBerry.

Then I paused, and knelt down by the dresser. I slid my hand beneath it and retrieved the dagger. The cold steel felt almost alive in my hands, aware in a way that no object should. I didn't like leaving any of the precious artifacts out of my possession, but more than that, I had a growing feeling that I'd need every weapon I could bring to hand—and soon. I slid the dagger into its sheath and put it into a side pocket on the backpack.

"You are wiser than you know, daughter," Shalizander whispered in my mind. *"There are many shadows inside the Vatican, many secrets kept and many bargains struck. You cannot trust anyone you meet there, and you must be wary of betrayal from anyone within its walls."*

"The Vatican didn't even exist when you were alive," I said. "What would you know about it?"

"Malkander was a priest, though not of the same faith. But all priests are essentially the same. They humble themselves before their god so that they might share in some of his power, while at the same time they work in devious ways behind each other's backs to gain in other, more worldly ways."

I took another glance around the room and decided I had everything I needed. *"So how do you explain Simon?"* I asked.

"He, too, seeks power in his own way, my daughter. Watch him today and learn."

I tried to find out more, but she went stubbornly silent. Which was typical—when I wanted her to shut up, she wouldn't. When I wanted her to talk, she kept quiet. She was about as cooperative as everyone else in my life seemed to be these days, but one thing was certain—I trusted Simon more than I did Shalizander.

"Trust is a costly commodity, Keeper," the Board of the Waters said. *"Especially where gods are concerned."*

"And what's *that* supposed to mean?" I asked.

"Keep the dagger close at hand," the Board

replied, its voice the distant gurgle of a mountain brook. *"Perhaps its keen edge will remind you to stay sharp when your heart tells you otherwise."*

"Vixisthra," I said, ordering them to silence. *"I'm getting sick of your riddles and your word games."*

"My agents tell me they are en route to the Library. I must admit, I'm looking forward to meeting the Keeper—the one that is supposed to fulfill the ultimate prophecy."

"Just be sure to keep your wits about you. Do not forget that she is searching for some of the most dangerous artifacts known to man, and their corrupting influence may be having a debilitating effect on her. I advise you to watch her closely, and note her mental and physical condition—if she is breaking under the strain, you may have to step in to help."

"I will keep that in mind during our meeting. Thank you so much for your wisdom in this matter."

"Please—it is the least I can do."

The sun was shining, and across the street, vendors were stocking their carts as I walked to the café where Simon was waiting. The air was cool, but not cold, and smelled vaguely of ginger.

Simon rose and gestured at the steaming cup across from him. "I took the liberty of ordering for you."

"Thanks." I pulled out the padded chair and sat down. "I need it."

"Do you want anything to eat?" he asked.

"Not right now—too nervous, I guess," I said, looking around. The table was set with a white cloth and a small vase of daisies, and I wondered if there were any restaurants left in the U.S. that felt like this place that was so open, and yet so intimate. Nearby, other diners were reading their morning papers or chatting, yet in some way it felt like Simon and I were the only ones here.

"You look more tired than usual, Jenna," Simon said. "Are you certain everything is okay?"

I bit back a sharp reply and nodded, sipping my coffee before replying. "I *am* tired. We've been moving non-stop since you showed up on my doorstep."

"I know," he said. "In fact, I've been thinking about something."

"Oh?"

"If you can hang in there until we find the Board of the Earth, we should be able to take a break," he said. "Maybe a week or two somewhere warm and quiet."

I looked at him over the rim of my cup. "Are you serious?"

"Aren't I always?" he said with a fleeting grin. "I'm not under half the strain you are, and *I'm* exhausted.

We don't know where the fifth Board is yet, and since no one else seems to have gotten this far, it's a good bet that it's quite safe for now."

I thought about it for a minute, and then said, "Lying low for a while would be a good thing for another reason, too. It might be nice to actually *think* about what we're going to do before we do it."

"Whatever happened to your sense of spontaneity?" he asked.

"It got left at home, along with a lot of other things," I muttered. "Anything I need to know before we head over to meet your fellow clergymen? I mean besides the obvious rules of no cursing, no taking the Lord's name in vain, no worshipping of idols, and no suggestive dancing."

Simon sighed and shook his head. "Those are the main points to avoid," he said. "You'll especially want to avoid the suggestive dancing part—there are elderly men in the Church who would likely drop dead in shock."

"It wouldn't be the *worst* way to go," I said. "I like to think I'm not *that* hard on the eyes, you know."

He smiled ruefully, and nodded. "I know."

It was funny how, since surviving our ordeals in Pompeii, we were finally able to talk like normal people. To laugh and smile and tease each other. It was almost as if, by admitting that we had feelings for each other—even if we couldn't act on them—we had, by mutual and unspoken consent, decided to be very good friends instead. It felt good to have an actual friend with me, rather than just a companion and chaperone.

We finished our coffees and Simon paid the bill. "Armand is expecting us at the Vatican library in half an hour. We can walk from here."

"That would be nice," I said. "I'd like to see more of the city."

"I don't know how much we'll get to see between here and there," he said. "But the wall that surrounds Vatican City is an impressive sight, and you should really walk up to it the first time you see it."

"Why do you say that?"

Simon was quiet for a moment, then he said, "Think about this. The Church is supposed to welcome people into the worship of Christ. Vatican City is the home of St. Peter's and the central seat of authority in the Christian world. Why do you suppose it's completely walled off?"

It was a good question, and I pondered it as we stepped into the springtime air of Rome and stretched our legs down old sidewalks crowded with bicycles and vendors and people walking to or from home and work. There was an odd vibrancy to the city, and it felt like I was walking along paths built over ancient roads. On every other corner, there was a magazine stand, and on the others there was always someone selling roasted nuts or skewered meat or coffee. At one point, Simon grabbed my arm and moved me out of the way as a young boy ran past, shouts following in his wake.

"What's that all about?" I asked.

"Gypsy," Simon said shortly. "They are everywhere here, and they send out their children as thieves to steal purses and wallets. They are like wolves, especially where tourists are concerned."

"How terrible!" I said, remembering the dream I'd had just before we left Pompeii. In it, I had been chased down dark tunnels by wolfish-looking men. "What kind of a life is that?"

"A tough one," he admitted, shrugging. "Perhaps they feel as though they have no other choice."

"There are always choices," I objected, thinking of my grandfather and how often he admonished me to know what my options were *before* choosing a path. But my grandfather hadn't known anything about the path that had been forced upon me after his death. I wondered what he would have had to say about all this.

"Naturally." Simon steered me gently around a cart selling fresh-roasted almonds. They smelled heavenly. "But the challenge is in seeing them, isn't it? Sometimes, the choices we have aren't always easily visible."

We crossed a busy street and turned a corner. Ahead of us, a massive wall loomed larger and larger as we approached, its gray brick almost black from years of rain and pollution. "Is that . . . ?"

Simon nodded. "The walls of Vatican City. It is independent of Rome and Italy, of course, a state unto itself. You can even get a postmark from there on a letter."

Our route led us along a sidewalk, with the wall

towering overhead on one side and a relatively nondescript street on the other. Looking up, I estimated that the barrier was at least sixty feet high. Maybe more. The bricks were pockmarked in numerous places. I pointed the marks out to Simon, and asked what they were from.

"Bullets, mostly," he said. "The areas where the walls were hit with cannon fire have long since been repaired."

I thought back to some of my history classes, and how often over the years the Church had also been a place of violence and death. "This place does have a rather bloody history, doesn't it?"

Simon smiled grimly. "That's one way to put it."

"Still, those wars are long past. Why keep the wall up in this day and age?"

"Maybe to keep people out," he said, "but I think it's just as likely there to keep us in. Or perhaps to remind us of our not always glorious past. I've never been quite sure myself. Perhaps after you've been inside, you'll have your own answer."

We walked past several wide and open entrances through the wall that had long lines of tourists, then stopped at a much less conspicuous door guarded by two very serious looking men in blue uniforms with a stylized symbol of a cross on them. Simon showed his credentials and spoke briefly in fluent Italian to them. The language was beautiful, even if I didn't know what they were saying. Finally, they waved us inside and Simon said, "Come on."

"Who are the guards?" I asked.

"The Swiss Guards," he said. "They've guarded Vatican City since 1506."

"I thought Switzerland was neutral."

"Not here," he replied. "Here they guard Vatican City and its inhabitants with something akin to zeal. Many have died over the years, protecting St. Peter's, the Pope, and other men of the Church."

The hall beyond the doors was very dark, like the bricks outside, but I followed him in anyway. We passed through it, and on the far side came out into a small courtyard with a fountain in the center. Stone-lined paths led to several different buildings.

"That way," Simon said, pointing, "leads to another courtyard, beyond which is the main museum—the one all the tourists get to see. We'll go this way." He started walking.

"And we're going to the library, right?"

"Actually, where we're going isn't open to the public," he said. "It's underground, beneath St. Peter's cathedral. A series of rooms in concentric rings. The center is actually directly below the altar itself."

"Why on earth would a library be kept beneath the church?"

"There are some things in the Vatican's private collection that are more . . . easily contained by the main seat of our faith."

I tried to imagine what objects and artifacts must be in such a place, and then dismissed it from my mind. It wasn't like I didn't have enough magic and mystery in my life. There wasn't any need to add to my bad dreams—and I suspected that whatever was hidden in the library could cause at least that.

"Jenna!" Father Andrew rose from his chair as I followed Simon into a room filled with rows of bookshelves. He took three long strides and wrapped me in his arms. "It's so good to see you, and know that you are safe."

In my head, I could hear the distant mutterings of the Boards in the Language of the Birds, but I squeezed my eyes shut and forced myself to ignore them. It wouldn't be good for Father Andrew to see me talking to myself.

"It's good to see you, too," I said, my voice muffled in his shoulder. This was the man who had christened me when I was born, who had presided over my religious education, had helped bury my parents and grandparents. He was from *home,* and at that moment, I suddenly knew how much I'd missed being there.

I finally stepped out of his embrace, and couldn't help but smile at him."You're looking well."

In truth, he looked worried, but about the same as always otherwise, with thinning blond hair and watery blue eyes behind his wire-rimmed glasses.

"And you," he said pointedly, "look tired."

Before I could reply, Armand walked into the room and greeted both Simon and myself. "I see you've already found Father Andrew," he added. "I don't think he's left the library since he arrived."

Armand was the leader of the Templar Knights as they existed today—not as Church enforcers, but as a secret society dedicated to the preservation of the Boards and the line of the Keepers. He had done a great deal to protect me in the past, and I knew I could trust him with my life.

It was unfortunate that there was a splinter group of Knights, until recently led by Peraud, whose goals were just the opposite. What would become of them now that Peraud was dead, I didn't know, but I held few illusions that they'd simply give up and go home.

We all exchanged greetings and pleasantries like we were friends who simply happened to meet here, rather than people all engaged in a search for dangerous magical artifacts. I looked around at the books, many of which were ancient tomes bound in cracked leather. "This isn't the one that the public gets to see, is it?" I asked Armand.

He laughed quietly. "No, it's not. There are volumes of lore and knowledge here that are forbidden to the public, and even off-limits to many members of the clergy. Father Andrew wouldn't normally be allowed within these walls, except for his experience in Miller's Crossing."

"Never forget that there are powers in the Vatican that seek us, Keeper," the Board of the Winds said. *"Be cautious in what you reveal here—especially to those you do not know and trust."*

"So how did *you* get in then?" I asked, trying to keep my voice light.

"As the leader of the Templar Knights, I am allowed certain latitude that others would not be. Much like you and Simon. Though I would not go so far as to say the relationship between the Knights and the Holy See has been totally repaired. We work together by necessity, rather than choice."

Remembering my history, I said, "Wasn't it a pope who originally disbanded the Knights?"

"And the king of France," Armand said. "Human men with human frailties and no understanding of what they were truly doing."

"Find out what the Vatican knows, daughter," Shalizander said. *"It may be the only way to prepare for whatever they will attempt."*

"Attempt?" I asked.

"They will want the power of the Boards for themselves," she said. *"Why else do you think they sent Simon, but to help you and to ensure that they have someone close by to secure the Boards for themselves."*

It was a disturbing point she raised, but I tried to put it out of my mind.

"Simon," Armand suggested, "why don't you come with me so you can bring me up to date? That will give Jenna and Father Andrew time to do their own catching up as well."

"Of course," he said. "We won't be long, Jenna."

I waved at them to go and made my way over to

a small trestle table stacked with books. "All this research can't be good for your eyes, Father."

Father Andrew chuckled. "It's not, Jenna," he said. "But it is fascinating. There have been events much like those that we experienced in Miller's Crossing throughout recorded history. Many have been deemed natural phenomena by Church investigators. Others, however, have not."

"Interesting," I said, keeping my voice neutral.

Father Andrew sat in the chair next to mine and took my hand, leaning in close enough to whisper. "Your secret is safe, Jenna," he said. "I have done nothing to confirm their suspicions, but be assured that the Vatican has had agents watching you and Simon's every move."

"Gently, daughter," Shalizander commanded. *"Trust is not a commodity brokered in the halls of faith."*

Trying to ignore her, I asked, "How much do they know—or think they know?"

"I'm not certain," he said. "They do know that you and Simon seek the Boards of Babylon. I don't believe they know how much success you have had."

"Do you?" I asked him.

"No," he said, "and I don't want to know. I owe my allegiance to the Mother Church and the Holy See, not to power-hungry cardinals." He squeezed my hand. "I'm more concerned about you, my dear. You look exhausted. Perhaps you should take some time away from all this."

Before I could answer, a door opened at the far end of the room and a small group of men dressed in the red robes of cardinals entered. One of them broke away and headed toward our table. He was tall and, broad-shouldered, with dark eyes and a direct gaze. His hair was the color of ashes, cropped short, and he had a strong jaw that jutted from his face like the prow of a ship.

Father Andrew and I stood as he approached, and Father Andrew gave a slight bow, but remained quiet.

"Father Andrew," the man said, his voice the smooth texture of honey. It sounded as though he would have made a fine singer. "I expect this is the guest you mentioned. Can I impose on you for an introduction?"

Seemingly startled, Father Andrew said, "Of course, of course." He gestured toward me. "Cardinal Cepheus, this is a very dear friend of mine, Jenna Solitaire."

Cardinal Cepheus turned to me and nodded, then extended his hand. "Miss Solitaire," he said in a deep voice. "It is a unique privilege to meet you. I have, of course, heard of you from Father Andrew and our own Simon Monk."

He expected me, I think, to kiss his hand as some traditions dictated, but instead I shook it firmly. "Cardinal," I said. "It's nice to meet you, too."

"He is a man of many faces and talents," Shalizander hissed. *"A wolf in shepherd's clothing."*

"Perhaps while you are here, we'll get the chance

to visit in more detail," he said. "I have heard something of the amazing events in your hometown, and I'd be most pleased to hear your version of them. The world is a strange and wondrous place."

"Be very wary, daughter. I recognize the taint of betrayal within him."

I mentally shook myself. I was jumping at shadows, and so was Shalizander. As far as she was concerned, everyone and everything was a potential threat to her goals. I had no reason to distrust Cardinal Cepheus. All he'd done was politely introduce himself.

"I'd like that," I said, thinking that the Cardinal seemed nice enough.

I had just decided to ask when he'd like to speak with me when Simon and Armand returned. Cepheus turned his attention to them, nodded to Armand, and smiled softly as he turned his gaze on Simon.

"Father Monk," he said. "I see you have returned to our precincts—and that the rumors of your return to the Faith are true as well. I am very pleased."

"Cardinal Cepheus," Simon replied, his voice cold and distant. "I never left the Faith, simply the title for a time. I'm surprised to find you here. One would normally expect to find you spending time at higher elevations than these drab surroundings. Surely his Holiness must find it difficult to do without your wise counsel."

"Do you see, my daughter? Listen to how they

fence with words, saying one thing and meaning quite another."

I realized that Simon had not used the proper title of "your Eminence," and knew instinctively that he'd done that on purpose. Then something strange happened.

Simon's face seemed to shift and change shape briefly, becoming almost triangular. Warping as though I was seeing him through water. I blinked and looked again, but he looked like he always did. Was I so tired that I'd begun hallucinating?

"I spend more time here than one might imagine, Father," Cepheus replied calmly. "There is a great deal of forgotten lore in these volumes—but you are already aware of this, I am certain."

Simon shrugged. "I've read most of them, yes," he said. "But the true value of their lore has yet to be determined, don't you think? So many of the stories are nothing more than illusions or outright lies."

"We shouldn't keep the Cardinal," Father Andrew said to Simon, obviously trying to keep things from getting out of hand. "He surely has better things to do than stand around down here and chat with us."

It was very clear that Simon and Cepheus knew each other, and that things could turn ugly very quickly. I watched them carefully, and then the same shift occurred in my vision, this time with Cepheus's face—only he looked more like an animal than a man.

I rubbed my eyes. I was overtired and overstressed. My mind was playing tricks on me.

I started to say something, but Armand spoke first.

"Simon!" he said, his voice carrying in the high-ceilinged room. "I'm positive that you and I have better things to do than to take up Cardinal Cepheus's valuable time."

Simon turned and looked at Armand, who was giving him a very direct gaze. "You're right, of course." He turned back to Cepheus. "I apologize . . . Your Eminence."

Cepheus smiled easily. "Think nothing of it, Father," he said. "From what I understand, you have been under a great deal of strain lately."

"Traveling the world isn't as much fun as one might think," Simon replied.

"Especially," Armand interjected, "when all those travels have borne so little fruit." His stare moved from Simon to me and then back again.

"See the tricks they play, daughter?" Shalizander asked. *"Each vying to say something while revealing nothing. They all play a very dangerous game."*

"It is a game of power, Keeper," the Board of the Waters added. *"Yet in comparison to what you would wield if you completed the ritual . . ."*

"Yes, the ritual," Shalizander said. *"Once our powers are combined—my magic and your mastery of the Boards . . ."*

". . . the defeat of small-minded enemies like

these would be of no consequence," the Board of Flames finished.

I tried to focus on the conversation, annoyed at the Boards and Shalizander. My head was pounding with a headache, and I was having difficulty telling which words were spoken in my mind, and which were being spoken aloud by the others.

"Vixisthra!" I shouted in my head, rubbing my temples.

Father Andrew was being respectfully quiet, while Armand and Simon stood there and told lies about our mission. No one had asked *me* about it, and *I* was the Keeper of the Boards. It was *my* life.

"They dismiss you, daughter, because they believe you to be in their power."

"You should show *them what you can do, Keeper."*

I heard Armand ask something about our next destination and Simon made a non-committal noise and muttered, "Northern Europe, I believe."

"What takes you there?" Cepheus asked. "Certainly, your expertise might be better suited to tasks here within the Holy See." He gestured expansively at the bookshelves. "So many mysteries yet to be solved."

"I do my best work on location, your Eminence," Simon said. "His Holiness—through intermediaries, of course—has expressed a desire that I continue on with my current work."

"And, of course," Armand interjected, "there is

still that matter of working with us to recover lost artifacts."

"They speak as if you are not even here, Keeper," the Board of the Winds said. *"As if it is they and not you who choose your destiny."*

I felt my teeth grinding together, and between the noise of the men talking and the Boards and Shalizander, it was simply too much. As I watched everyone's face morphed and changed, then changed back again. Simon. Cardinal Cepheus. Armand. Even Father Andrew's features warped and twisted into a mockery of his gentle expression.

The pressure built in my head, squeezing out everything—thought, awareness, vision—and I had to stop it before I exploded.

"Vixisthra!" I shouted. "Just stop it! Shut up! Shut up all of you!"

The room fell utterly silent as everyone turned and stared at me, and I realized that my words had been shouted out loud and not in my head.

Both Armand and Simon began to speak, even as Father Andrew put a comforting hand on my shoulder. I shrugged it off angrily, and then Cepheus spoke, cutting the other two off. "Gentlemen, you will excuse us, please."

Everyone, myself included, looked at him like he'd grown a second head.

"I'm sorry," I said, wondering if I was going completely mad. "I am . . . very tired."

"Obviously," Cepheus continued smoothly, "this young lady is in some distress. She is clearly exhausted, and our prattling is not helping matters in the slightest. Indulge me, please, and allow me to counsel her privately."

I saw Simon's eyes widen, but I nodded my agreement. If nothing else, I thought, perhaps the Cardinal's soothing voice would ease my headache, if not my troubles.

"They are still meeting in the archives, but they'll be leaving soon, I imagine."

"And?"

"Our meeting was not as fruitful as I had hoped. Simon and Armand are definitely hiding something—I suspect that she is further along in the quest than I suspected. I have sent agents to keep an eye on them. I wish to see where they are headed."

"An excellent idea. Keep me informed as to their progress, and I will also do what I can to help from this end."

Cardinal Cepheus turned to me. His dark, compelling eyes bore into mine. "You are, I understand, of the faith, Miss Solitaire?"

"It . . . it's been a long time, your Eminence," I muttered. I was confused, and didn't know what to say. At least the hallucinations had stopped for the moment.

"Allow an old cardinal a few moments of time to talk with you," he said. "Please."

"I . . . of course," I said.

"Gentlemen?" the cardinal said, making a vague gesture with his hand. "I'm sure you can fill your time for a few moments in the meeting room, yes?"

Armand, Father Andrew, and Simon headed for the small meeting room where the cardinals had come from earlier. Simon risked one glance back at me and his eyes were filled with warnings. He put a finger to his lips in a "be quiet" gesture, and it was all I could do not to send him a much less polite gesture in return.

Gently taking my elbow, Cardinal Cepheus led me to the table where Father Andrew had been studying. He pushed the stacks of books aside and pulled out a chair for me.

"Please sit down, young lady," he said. "You are clearly under great deal of stress. I have no doubt that at least some of that is young Father Monk's fault. He works very hard, and his companions are often driven to the edge of exhaustion by his travels."

Feeling a little like a schoolgirl, I sat down and stared at my hands, saying nothing.

After a few moments of awkward silence, Cardinal Cepheus said, "I understand that you've been traveling with Father Monk for some time now."

Just hearing Simon called "Father" sounded odd to my ears, but I was well aware that the hierarchy of the Church demanded such formality among them. I nodded. "Since early spring."

"Traveling around the world on the schedule

you've been keeping isn't easy, I'm sure," he said. His soothing voice was helping to dispel my headache, I realized. Or maybe it was just that there weren't so many voices all at once.

"And Father Monk deals in . . . often difficult-to-understand situations," he continued. "Sometimes even dangerous situations."

"He can take care of himself," I said. "He's proven that much anyway."

"Oh, I have no illusions about that," Cepheus said, smiling. "While his commitment to the faith may lack true belief or zeal, his ability to defend himself has never been questioned."

Stunned, I did my best to hide my reaction. Simon *was* a man of true faith. I knew this because I'd seen him heal Tom while he had been dying in the hospital back home. I knew it because even though he wanted more than a friendship with me, he refused to cross those boundaries, and I knew it because . . . well, because I felt it. Even more than I did standing next to Father Andrew. Or this man.

When I didn't reply, the cardinal said, "But I have no desire to discuss Father Monk. I'm more concerned with you now. How can I help you with your burdens?"

"Use caution, daughter," Shalizander said. *"This man radiates . . . hunger."*

"It's too bad the Language of the Birds doesn't keep you *quiet,"* I said. *"Imagine how much better my life would be if that were the case."*

"In time, you will come to appreciate my counsel."

Ignoring her, I said, "Thank . . . thank you for your concern, your Eminence. I'll be fine. I'm afraid I'm overtired, and should have stayed at the hotel to rest today."

"When you're young, it's easy to overestimate what you can and can't do," he said. "I understand that you and Father Monk are seeking the so-called Boards of Babylon together. His reports indicate that your family is connected to them somehow?"

If only you knew a tenth of what I know.

"I guess so," I said, wondering where he was going with this line of questioning. "There's a lot we don't know yet."

There, I thought. *That's a nice, meaningless statement.*

"Magic, as you know, is forbidden by the Church. Many of its artifacts are simple scams, designed to trick the mind with illusion. Still . . ." his voice trailed off thoughtfully.

"Still?" I asked.

"Some are possibly dangerous. I wouldn't like to imagine that Father Monk had put you in any danger by not turning them over to proper Church authority, should they be found."

"This is closer to his true desire, Keeper," the Board of the Waters said. *"He wants the Boards for himself."*

"I understand your concern, your Eminence." I shrugged. "Unfortunately, all of our travels so far have only led to phantoms and ancient history, rather than the Boards themselves."

He looked disappointed, but hid it well. "In that case, would you accept a word of advice from an old man?"

I nodded, keeping my face neutral.

"Take some time off from your journeys with Simon. Rest here in Rome and see the sights. There will always be more work to do."

"I'll . . . take that under consideration," I said. "Thank you."

The cardinal stood then and once more offered his hand. This time, I followed the form and kissed his signet ring, while the Boards and Shalizander all shrieked an objection in my mind and set off my headache again.

"He deserves anything but *empty gestures of faith, daughter!"* Shalizander said.

"The Keeper of the Boards bows to no one!" the Boards cried in unison.

He crossed the room and opened the door, gesturing for the others to rejoin us. Once they did, he said, "I'm afraid I'm required elsewhere at the moment, but I hope to see you again, Miss Solitaire."

"I'm sure we will," I said.

"Armand, Father Monk, Father Andrew." The cardinal nodded at them, then left the room.

As soon as he was gone, the three men clustered around me.

"What did he want, Jenna? What did he say?" Armand asked.

"He's very interested in what Simon and I are doing. He knows we're searching for the Boards, and suspects that Simon hasn't told the—how did he put it?—'proper Church authorities' of our findings."

"That settles it," Armand said. "We've got to get the two of you out of the city as soon as possible."

"We can't trust him," Simon said. We'd left the Vatican, and found a small *trattoria* a few blocks away. "I've never had any proof, but there's something about that man that feels untrustworthy. It's like looking at a snake."

"You don't trust anyone," I said. "He was perfectly polite, Simon, even when you were rude. He didn't say anything to me that was other than concerned."

The waiter appeared as we sat down and everyone ordered a beverage.

"Jenna may be right in this case, Simon," Armand said. "I've never heard anything about Cardinal Cepheus to cause alarm. He's power hungry, of course, but that's only natural in a man who has risen to his rank within the Church."

"Believe what you want," Simon said, "but there's something about him—"

"Perhaps," Father Andrew suggested, "your distrust comes from your dealings with him when you first came into your position."

"I figured you two knew each other," I said. "What happened?"

Simon scowled as Armand grinned. "They argued constantly," he said. "At the time, Cepheus was a rapidly rising monsignor, soon to be a bishop, and was in charge of the Vatican's special collections—part of which we were sitting in back there."

"What are the special collections anyway?"

"The vast majority of the items that we worked with," Simon answered, "are books relating to the occult. Obviously, some artifacts as well." He took a sip of his lemon water. "There are other collections, of course, but everything we worked with involved the occult in some way."

"So what happened after you arrived?" I asked, wondering what the other artifacts were and then deciding I had enough problems with my own.

"Simon came here with a chip on his shoulder about the size of a truck," Armand said. "Don't even try to deny it, my friend. He was knowledgable, and a genius at unlocking ancient mysteries, but in those early years, it was Cepheus who taught him, not the other way around. Simon didn't respond well to his tutelage."

I caught myself smiling. It was rare to hear anything about Simon's past, and this little glimpse into his early life in the Church was intriguing. "Are you saying he was—" I paused, as though thinking very hard, then added, "—arrogant?"

Armand and Father Andrew both laughed while Simon continued to frown.

"Enough with the ancient history," Simon said. "We need to stay focused, regardless of whether Cepheus can be trusted or not."

"Agreed," Armand said, though his smile remained as he turned to me. "Where do we go from here, Jenna? Simon mentioned something about Scotland?"

I nodded and relayed my vision of the wizard Emrys from the night before, trying to include as many details as possible, down to the landscape, the stones and even Coghlan's demise.

"The only problem," I finished, "is that I have no idea who Emrys might have been, or even where to begin looking for this phoenix stone. I don't even know exactly *what* it is. Scotland's large enough that just wandering around isn't going to do the trick."

"Have you been able to sense the Board of the Earth at all?" Armand asked.

"No," I said, shaking my head. "I've tried a couple of times but haven't been able to. Maybe it's the noise from the other Boards, or maybe it's something else."

"Jenna," Simon said. "Are you certain the name was Emrys?"

"Yes," I said. "Positive."

"That wasn't his only name," Simon said, a rare smile appearing on his face. "Emrys means 'immortal.' Most people know him by a more common name in all the books and movies. That name was Merlin."

"Don't be ridiculous," Father Andrew said. "Merlin is just a legend, a myth."

Simon chuckled. "So most people believe," he said. "But in every legend and myth, there's a nugget or two of truth. Much scholarly research has been done on this subject, and a number of the treatises conclude that there really was a man named Merlin. Variously, he's been depicted as a druid, an engineer, and—of course—a wizard."

"Are you saying," I asked, "that Merlin the Magician was real? And that he is Emrys?"

"Not exactly," Simon said. "I'm suggesting that *if* those scholars are right, the possibility exists. It would make a certain amount of sense."

"So where do we find his grave?" I asked.

Simon reached into his briefcase and pulled out a sheaf of papers. "I . . . appropriated these from the library this morning," he said, "while you were talking to Cepheus. I didn't think they'd be of interest so soon, but was planning on using them for when we went after the fifth Board."

"Thinking so far ahead, Simon?" I asked. "Pretty soon, we'll be having full-on planning sessions before we embark on an adventure."

He shrugged. "You've mentioned that before," he said. "I thought studying these might be helpful at some point. It seems that we continue to find the Boards at places of special interest, historically speaking."

Armand leaned forward, his eyes gleaming with interest. "I think that's called 'stealing,' Simon, and

I'm pretty sure there's a commandment against it."

"I think of it as 'borrowing,'" Simon said. "I'll return them when I'm done." He shrugged. "Besides, all the commandments are basically about stealing anyway."

"How do you figure?" Armand asked.

"Murder is theft of life, adultery is theft of spouse, idolatry is theft of God," Simon started explaining, but I cut him off.

"Excuse me, but could we stay on topic? What do you have there, Simon?"

"Sorry," he said. "You're right." He held up the papers. "These are a collection of maps. But more specifically, they are maps of the locations of ancient myths and legends. Maps where things *might* have occurred."

"Handy," Armand said.

"It's not very accurate," Simon admitted. "But I've done a fair amount of research on Arthurian legend over the years—mostly because of the Grail. What Emrys told you was that the Picts took the stone to mark a battlefield. While there were many battles in those days, I can only imagine one where Emrys, if he's truly Merlin, would have been with the phoenix stone." He flipped the pages until he came to a map of Scotland, and pointed to a small black dot. "That is the Scottish Highlands, and the black dot is Camallan."

Thinking of the movies, I said, "Don't you mean Avalon or Camlan or Camelot?"

"No," Simon said. "The real name was Camallan.

Scholars suggest that it's probably where King Arthur and Merlin made their final stand—and it could be the site of their graves."

"*If* any of it is true at all," Armand said. "There's an awful lot of legend and oral tradition mixed into your theory, Simon. There's no actual proof that Arthur, let alone Merlin, even existed."

"Actually, there is some that suggests the core story—a hard-pressed war leader who fought off the Picts and the Celts for many years—has its basis in fact. The names may have been different, but the basics are there for sure." He shrugged. "Besides, do you have any better ideas?"

"Not really," Armand admitted. "But why go off on a wild-goose chase if it will gain us nothing?"

"For once the priest is correct, daughter," Shalizander said. *"As I told you before, you must journey to that place in order to get the next Board. The Emrys was a very powerful wizard, and his magic transcends time—much like mine."*

"I think Simon's right," I said. "If nothing else, maybe the phoenix stone is there, even if Merlin and Arthur aren't anything but ghosts and old stories. But 'we' don't have to do anything. Only Simon and I have to go."

"That's true," Armand said. "And I can help by going to England. Glastonbury Tor houses a great deal of Arthurian lore, and perhaps I'll be able to find more concrete clues there to guide us."

"And I'll stay here to keep an eye on things," Father Andrew said. "It would be best not to arouse the cardinal's suspicions—in case Simon turns out to be right."

"Simon takes paranoia to a whole new level," I said. "But you'll be safe here, and that's as good a reason as any I can think of."

"Then it's decided," Armand said. "I'll take care of our travel arrangements, while the two of you go pack. I shouldn't have any trouble getting you flights out by tomorrow morning at the latest."

"The sooner the better," Simon said. "We need to keep moving."

"Tomorrow," Father Andrew said, his voice firm and brooking no argument. "Give Jenna a night to sleep."

Simon looked at me and I saw true sadness in his eyes.

"She doesn't sleep anymore, Father, not like you and I do," he said. "Nor does she dream like you and I dream."

I remembered Emrys's suggestion that once I had all the Boards of the Elements, many of my problems would go away. That I would be able to control them better.

"But someday I will," I said softly. "Someday soon."

"I hope so," Simon said. "No one should fear sleep."

"I don't fear it, Simon," I said. "I'm just sick of not getting any."

"The ritual, daughter," Shalizander said, *"would make those problems disappear even sooner, and*

make your control over the Boards more complete."

"Yes, Keeper," the Boards said. *"The ritual would help."*

"Vixisthra," I said to them. Even my mental voice sounded worn out.

"My men have followed them to Scotland. They've holed up in a hotel for the evening, and are being watched even now. It's obvious, however, that they're tracking one of the Boards."

"Didn't Simon mention something about the next one being in northern Europe?"

"It may still be, but I think they're farther along than we suspect. I think its time to get a closer look at what Jenna and Simon are really doing."

"I advise caution—after all, you don't want to tip your hand too early."

"My operatives know what they're doing."

"Perhaps, but they've never encountered anything like this before."

A light rain fell as Simon and I boarded a flight from Rome to Edinburgh early the next morning. The day was drab and gray, and the mist made the brick of the older buildings look like they were crying.

Even though it was a fairly short flight—about

four hours—Armand had purchased first-class seats, and I did my best not to smile at Simon's scowl as we found them.

"Think of it as a little bonus for all the hard work we do," I said. "We stay in cheap hotels, never take a break, risk our lives on a nearly daily basis, and in return we get to fly first class."

"It's still wasteful," Simon said, putting his black canvas duffel bag in the overhead compartment.

I slid my backpack under my seat and leaned back into the chair. "But much more comfortable," I said. "Besides, I'd rather talk about something else."

Simon sat down and asked if I'd gotten any sleep the night before. I shook my head.

"I didn't even really try," I admitted. "I read for a little bit—not the Chronicle, in case you were wondering—but mostly I just stared at the walls and waited for sunrise. I may have dozed for a few minutes."

He sighed and shook his head. "Jenna, I know that sleeping is difficult for you right now, but even broken sleep is better than none at all. If you never let your body rest, you'll get sick, and be much more susceptible to the Boards' influence."

I shrugged noncommittally. It wasn't like the Boards gave me a break anyway, and getting sick seemed unlikely, too. For all I knew, Shalizander and the Boards could keep me on my feet even if I was dead. And probably would, if it meant getting their way. "I don't really want to talk about my sleep habits either."

"What's on your mind?" he asked.

I hesitated for a moment, then said, "Shalizander."

Simon raised his eyebrows. "That's a heavy topic. What about her?"

I didn't want to burden him with her current desire, or even the fact that she was still alive. "I'd like to know more about her," I said. "She started all this after all."

"You probably know more about her than I do," he admitted. "From reading the Chronicle if nothing else. But I have a thought, if you'd like to hear it."

"Sure," I said. The plane began to taxi toward the runway, and I popped a piece of gum into my mouth. Fresh breath and help popping my ears during takeoff—a double benefit.

"I think," Simon began, "that she was somehow misled. Maybe that's all any of us will be able to say when we are seated beneath the throne of judgment, but if I were to guess, she didn't make the Boards with the intention of creating all this."

"What makes you think that?"

"A guess," he replied. "If she'd truly intended to make them this way, why bother to hide them at all? Why not keep them for herself?" He shook his head. "No, I think someone misled her about the magic used in creating the Boards, perhaps betrayed her. Maybe she believed she was creating something good."

I thought about it for a minute. If she had been betrayed, would that explain her madness? So many years waiting for the fulfillment of a prophecy to make things right again could drive anyone insane. It was an interesting idea, but it seemed a little naïve to me, and I said so.

Simon smiled, and I was struck anew by how handsome he was, how his smile softened the lines in his face. "Maybe so," he said. "But I think *most* people are good, Jenna. Most people want to do the right thing. Often, confusion and desperation lead to poor judgment."

"You're very sweet," I said. "I hope you're right."

I closed my eyes, hoping to get some rest. But shortly after takeoff, Simon put down his cup of horrible-smelling airplane coffee and said, "Speaking of heavy topics, I think there's something else you should know."

"Uh-oh," I said. "Usually this means bad news."

"Not necessarily," he said. "But I think it's possible, even likely, that the Vatican has assigned other agents to finding the Boards. Cardinal Cepheus practically vowed to keep an eye on us, and that means he's sending his own people into the field. He wouldn't hesitate to take all of the Boards, if he could."

"What makes you think that?" I asked. I thought about what Father Andrew had said about our being closely watched by other agents within the Vatican. I wondered if he had told Simon about his suspicions or if it was something he'd come up with on his own.

"You only saw a tiny portion of the Vatican's

special collections. Many objects of arcane interest are kept in even more secure vaults for 'safekeeping.' Ancient texts are just one thing that interests them. Their true interest is in keeping objects of power and the knowledge of such powers out of the hands of those who are unable to handle them."

"That's a pretty arrogant attitude," I said. "How do they decide who can and can't handle such things?"

Simon's eyes flashed. "They don't," he said. "They just assume that they are the only ones qualified to do so."

"You don't agree?" I asked.

"It is not my place to make such judgments."

"But you did with me," I objected. "You could have told Cardinal Cepheus that we already had the first three Boards."

"You are a special case," Simon said. "Cepheus believes he understands the nature of the Boards, and he very well might." Simon's tone made it clear that he didn't believe what he was saying for an instant. "But I don't trust him."

"Why?" I asked. "It was clear that you two didn't like each other, but what's the history besides the chip on your shoulder story Armand told us?"

Simon sighed heavily. "Cepheus wields a great deal of power and influence in the Holy See, and even with his Holiness. Those that cross him often pay a heavy price. We must be very cautious about who we trust, Jenna—even when their motives *appear* to be pure."

"Even Father Andrew?"

"I think," Simon said, "that we can trust him, if anybody, why?"

I decided to share Father Andrew's suspicions. "Because he believed that other people in the Vatican were keeping an eye on us, too."

Simon seemingly took this in stride, and nodded. "It's a safe bet."

I tried to press him for more information on Cardinal Cepheus, but he wouldn't say any more. Finally I gave up and turned my attention to the passing landscape below us, trying to remember details from the dream I'd had of Merlin Emrys. I thought it might be possible to recognize details from the terrain, but that seemed very silly—surely a great deal had changed since the time of Arthur! Still, it was a slim hope, which was better than none at all.

Periodically, the Boards or Shalizander would speak to each other or me, sometimes in English, sometimes in the Language of the Birds, mostly the latter. The words were the usual babble of oddly combined consonants and syllables that made up the language of men before the fall of the Tower of Babel.

I got the impression they were plotting another strategy to convince me to complete the dagger ritual, and that was more than a little disturbing. Sooner or later, they might come up with a method or reason for me to do it, and then . . . I wasn't completely certain I'd even be myself anymore.

I had spent more than enough time watching horror movies, reading books, and listening to the Catholic Church to be absolutely terrified of being possessed—and what Shalizander wanted, I believed, was a form of possession, nothing less. In retrospect, I knew it was this fear that had given me the strength to master the Board of the Winds when it tried to destroy my hometown.

It was one thing to be the so-called Daughter of Destiny, to be the Keeper of the Boards and deal with all the problems of that, but I was still *me*, too. I was Jenna Solitaire, first and foremost, and there were lines I would not cross.

These thoughts consumed me for the rest of the flight, while Simon appeared engrossed in an old book he'd brought along on Arthurian legend.

After landing and customs, we headed for the luggage area for our bags. While waiting, I fired up my BlackBerry and checked my e-mail. It had been a few days since I'd heard from my best friends back home, and I was happily surprised to find a note from Kristen Evers.

Happy, anyway, until I read it:

Dear Jenna,

I hope this finds you safe and well, and I don't want to add to your burdens, but I don't know where else to turn. Have you heard from Tom at all?

A few nights ago, Tom and I had a disagreement and he left. He's been driving on his own for the last couple of weeks, and I thought he'd come back after he cooled off, but he didn't. He hasn't come back, and I'm so worried.

Tom hasn't been himself lately, and he's so angry all the time. I don't know what to do, Jenna, so if you've heard from him, please let me know as soon as possible.

Your friend,

Kristen

Confused, I paged back through my e-mails until I found the last one from Tom, which I hadn't had a chance to read yet. The first part of it read:

Dear J.—

I hope you're well and that Father Andrew was able to get in touch, too. This is going to sound crazy, but I'm sending this from a new account, and please don't tell Kristen I've been in touch with you. She's . . . I don't know what she's doing, but she's not acting like herself at all.

One day, she talks about how much she misses you and wishes this would all end so you could come home and then next she's muttering in her sleep about undeserved power and the eye. It's all very strange. I don't know where we go from here, I really don't. Every time I try to talk to her about it, she snaps at me and tells me I'm imagining things or being paranoid.

After that, it was his usual pleasantries.

Simon must have seen the concern on my face, because he quit his intent perusal of the luggage conveyor and asked what was wrong.

"I don't know," I said. "Something's going on between Tom and Kristen." I showed him Tom's e-mail, then Kristen's.

"That is strange."

"I don't know what to believe," I said. "Kristen sounds perfectly rational to me, and Tom does, too." I wondered what was really going on, and even with everything else that was on my plate, my first thought was to get back on a plane and head home.

Spotting our luggage, Simon grabbed it. "Jenna, you can't work out their problems for them. We have more important work to do here than mediate a lovers' spat."

I felt my teeth clench at Simon's dismissive attitude, then realized I was overreacting. Too little sleep and too much stress. Still, I asked, "How do you know it's just a lovers' spat? What if something is really wrong?"

"Perhaps you're right," Simon said. "And I'm sorry. But the most likely possibility is that Tom is just adjusting to his new life. I've met and spoken with many people who deal with paralysis, and one of the consistent things I've heard is that there comes a point where all their emotions really boil down to extreme anger."

"He didn't sound angry in his e-mail to me," I said.

"No, he didn't," he admitted. "But Tom's sensitive and intelligent enough to know that you already have your hands full."

"Daughter," Shalizander said in my mind, *"there is no time for this right now. The next Board awaits."*

The Boards chorused their agreement, and I sighed in resignation.

"You're probably right," I said to Simon.

Still, there was no point in telling Kristen everything either. Tom had a right to expect that I would respect his request for privacy. I quickly tapped out a reply to her.

Dear Kristen,

I'm sorry to hear that you and Tom are having difficulties. I wish I could tell you that I've heard from him, but I haven't in quite some time. The last message I received from him was when I was still in Pompeii.

I'll do my best to find him, including sending a note to Father Andrew, and if I hear anything at all I'll let you know. Please do the same for me, okay?

I've got to run, but I'll check e-mail as often as I can. Try to take care of yourself, Kristen, and not to worry too much. Tom is more than capable—even in a wheelchair—of taking care of himself.

Your friend,

Jenna

"Better?" Simon asked after I hit the SEND button.

"It will have to do," I said. "Until I can figure out what's really going on."

"I think my paranoia is starting to rub off on you," he chided. "Just because our lives are filled with dangerous enemies and magic doesn't mean everyone else's is."

"That's the part that Tom probably doesn't know about yet," I said. "And you don't either."

"What?" he asked, his eyes suddenly concerned.

"Kristen is a practicing witch. She has been for years. That's how she got Tom to fall for her to begin with."

Simon opened his mouth to say something, then apparently thought better of it and snapped it shut again. Finally, he settled on, "Are you serious?"

"Very much so," I said. "She told me before we left."

"Why didn't you say anything before now?"

"Why should I have? It's not like she's out there

sacrificing virgins and dancing naked under the moon and drinking blood! This is Kristen we're talking about. She's as sweet and wonderful as anyone I've ever known."

Simon hefted his suitcase and mine and stalked out of the airport. I grabbed my backpack and followed him outside. The weather was unchanged from when we'd left Rome. The sky was gray and a light drizzle fell, making the concrete black and slick. It was colder here than it had been in Rome, and I was glad to have my new coat with me.

He didn't speak until we were in the back of a cab and on our way to our hotel, then he turned to me and said very softly, "Jenna, witches tamper with very serious powers—spirits and elementals and mystic energies not unlike those of the Boards. Not all of those powers are goodness and light, as you well know."

Startled by his intensity, I said, "And?"

"And what if she's tampered with something beyond her control—and now it's controlling her?"

The thought had never crossed my mind, and I felt a little taken aback by the notion. "But . . ." I started to say, then realized I was about to defend Kristen when I didn't really know all that much about what kind of witch she was.

"But?"

I sighed. "I never thought of it like that. She could be in real trouble, couldn't she?"

"Very much so, I'm afraid," he said. "Why do

you think the Vatican takes such items into its special collection? To keep them out of the hands of the uninitiated. To keep people safe."

"I thought it was to—well, I don't really know what I thought."

"She could be in very grave danger, Jenna," he said. "See if you can find out what's really going on with them, before it's too late."

I nodded, my thoughts of home stronger than ever before. How could I help them from here?

"You can't," Shalizander said. *"And that, too, is part of the burden you carry."*

Dear Tom—

Where are you? What's going on?

I got a note from Kristen that said you two had a fight and that you left. She said she hasn't seen you in three days. I didn't tell her about your e-mail, but please write and let me know you're okay.

Your friend,

Jenna

Dear Father Andrew—

Please excuse the shortness of this note.

If you happen to hear from Tom, will you tell him to contact me? I think there may be a problem between him and Kristen.

Jenna

I shut down the BlackBerry and returned it to my backpack, then stretched out on the bed. It had been a long day between the flight and getting to the hotel and finding a place to eat. My first take of this country was that there were far more forms of *haggis*—the traditional dish of Scotland—than should be allowed by law.

Even Simon, for all his world travel, settled for something less revolting than the organs of a sheep mixed with various spices and then boiled in a stomach. I didn't have much of an appetite to begin with and my mistake of asking for an explanation of the dish didn't add to it one bit.

Still, we found a restaurant that served fresh seafood and had a quiet meal, then a walk back to the hotel. We planned to get a good night's rest and then drive to the Highlands the next day to look for Camallan and the phoenix stone. Simon politely escorted me to my room, then bid me goodnight, saying something about having more research to do before we left.

I was worried about Tom and Kristen, and even more worried that the Boards and Shalizander had all been relatively quiet during the day. As tempting as it was to think they were giving up, I knew it was only the calm before the storm.

I took a quick shower, changed into my baggy

sweats and a t-shirt, and climbed into bed. If nothing else, I thought, maybe the calm would last long enough for me to get some sleep.

This faint hope followed me as I closed my eyes—and ended just as quickly.

The Tower thrusts up into the sky like a giant's finger created from red bricks. Inside, I look through an opening that may have been a window once. The landscape below is blasted and empty. Here and there, faint outlines of where buildings once stood, where the ancient, glorious hanging gardens once grew, are the only signs that there was ever anything else here besides the Tower.

It is a scene from a post-apocalyptic movie. Nothing lives here. Nothing could.

I turn from the window as the first scream echoes in the still, dead air. It is a scream of utter despair, a scream of defeat and desperation. Steps lead upward and I follow them, the only sounds my footfalls on the stone and the occasional piercing cry of whomever is being tortured above. That is the sound, I realize. It is the sound someone makes when they are being tortured.

There are no other exits as the stairs twist around the outside wall of the Tower. Near the top is a landing and a closed door. The door bears the marks of an old fire, scorched and charred, the wood warped from whatever intense heat was applied to it. Some-

how, it still fits within its frame. I turn the blackened handle as another scream shatters the silence.

The room beyond is simple and spare—a single bed sits against one wall, a desk and workbench near another. And there is the man whose screams pulled me up the steps.

For a long minute, my eyes are caught by the image of Simon, bound by chains to two heavy old planks. Stunned, I move closer and realize that the man is not Simon, but my old enemy, Peraud—Simon's twin brother. Slightly shorter and a bit heavier, it would be difficult to tell them apart, but I have seen his face too many times not to know the difference with the eyes in my heart, even when those in my head want to fool me.

He is stripped to the waist and blood runs freely down his savaged body. For a moment I think wolves have mauled him, and I remember the dream I had just before leaving Pompeii. A dream of wolves chasing me down dark tunnels.

His eyes are closed and his breathing is ragged and faltering.

I step into the room and see a simple chair near a window, with a small table next to it. Seated in the chair is Shalizander. My ultimate grandmother. She wears a plain white cotton gown, with a belt of gold wrapped around her waist. She appears to be only a little older than I am. She sips a glass of wine as if sitting in a garden for tea, and then her gaze meets mine.

Her eyes are ancient, and reveal the thousands

of years she has suffered, trapped in here—that, and more than a hint of madness.

"Hello, daughter," she says. "I've tried to convince you nicely, but your stubborn nature has proven to me that perhaps a more serious demonstration will be required. It's time you grew up a bit." She gestured at Peraud's broken form. "What do you think of my handiwork?"

"What are you doing to him?" I ask, appalled that she is so casual about destroying another person like one would throw a napkin away.

"When you stabbed Peraud with my dagger, his magical shields were shattered—paltry little things that they were—and it opened a door for me. Not much, mind you, but enough to gain a small foothold in his mind and on his soul. When his master, Malkander, ended his life, I took his spirit and brought it here."

"Why?" I ask. "To what purpose?"

She shrugged and pushed her hair—so much like mine—over her shoulder.

"For revenge—after all, you are my daughter," she says. "And also for fun. I haven't had a new plaything in a long time."

I shudder and suddenly feel cold, though the air here is warm and humid.

"What did he ever do to you?" I ask. "If anyone had a reason to want revenge on him, it was me—and I don't. Knowing he's dead is satisfaction enough."

Peraud moans and his breathing begins to hitch. He is dying. Again.

"He tried to harm you, daughter," she says, a small smile playing around the corners of her mouth. "I should think you'd be pleased."

"Hardly," I say. "How long has he been here?"

"Only a few days, as time is reckoned in the mortal realm," she replies. "Though I imagine it feels like much, much longer to him." She waved a negligent hand and Peraud screamed once more, his eyes snapping open. All his wounds were healed.

Peraud's haunted eyes find mine, and in them I can see the ghosts of failure. "I thought I heard your voice," he says. "Have you come to gloat at your victory, Keeper?"

I shake my head, stunned by Shalizander's powers—and her willingness to use them this way.

"I don't really hold grudges, Peraud," I say. "And I don't condone torture, not even of my enemies."

"You aren't quite the heir Shalizander expected, are you?" he asked. "She must be disappointed."

"Quiet, fool," Shalizander snaps. "Or would you like me to start again?"

Peraud's mouth snaps closed, and she turns her attention back to me.

"This is a simple diversion, daughter," she says. "Of no real meaning or consequence. I brought you here to discuss other things."

Forcing my gaze away from Peraud, I ask, "Such as?"

"It is time for you to complete the ritual of the dagger. My powers are all that stand between you and certain failure. Sooner or later, Malkander or

one of his many minions will kill you, and his *prophecy will come to fruition, rather than ours."*

"His prophecy?"

"There are two sides to every coin, daughter. There is light and shadow, male and female, positive and negative. In the same moment I uttered my prophecy, Malkander uttered his." She smiles grimly. "It goes without saying that his prophecy presents a much less desirable outcome for mankind."

"I've never heard either one," I say. "At least not the full version. Care to enlighten me?"

She laughs. "Not yet, daughter. In due time—and only after you have completed the ritual."

"And if I don't?" I ask. "I don't want to be possessed."

She mutters a few words under her breath and a shimmering field appears in the air between us. "Look into the mirror, my daughter," she says.

Compelled by her words and her magic, I do. My face stares back at me. My eyes are red and tired, with dark circles beneath them. There are lines on my face that hadn't been there when all of this started. I look older than I really am.

"If you don't complete the ritual, you will die," Shalizander says. "If Malkander and his ilk don't destroy you, the Boards soon will. Already, you are at the very edge of your endurance and abilities. With my assistance, the voices and the powers of the Boards will be controlled, limited to what I deem required of them."

I stare into the mirror and see how exhausted I

look. How beaten. I wonder if Shalizander is right, and the only way is to complete the ritual and allow her spirit a place within my own body, my own mind. I wonder if she is lying merely because she wants *to live again?*

As if she were reading my mind, Shalizander says, "I am capable of lying, daughter, but I'm not about this. The bloodline has grown too thin, the magic in your blood too weak. My powers, on the other hand, have only strengthened with time. Together, we can defeat Malkander. Otherwise, your death—and that of your world—is certain."

I turn from her to Peraud, who watches us intently. There is a message in his eyes, a promise, but I cannot fathom what it might be.

"I'll think about it," I say, turning back to her.

"Decide quickly," she says. "Time is running out. Should you attempt to take on the burden of the fourth Board, or the master Board itself, your mind will shatter like flawed crystal."

I begin to reply, but she suddenly raises a hand and says, "You must go now. There are intruders entering your room. Protect the Boards and destroy them!"

I feel myself jerked backward and down, away from the Tower and it quickly disappears from view. I hurtle through darkness and light.

Returning to my body and my hotel room, her words follow me like an echo I cannot escape.

"Destroy them!"

"I think we've spent enough time waiting. My agents will take her tonight."

"You are moving prematurely, I think. Patience is our best ally in this matter."

"She is nothing but a young girl with a trinket she barely understands. Once she's in custody, we'll force her to take us to the next Board, and then we'll have them all."

"Are you sending your best *men?"*

"Of course. Why?"

"Because replacing your best *men will be expensive and time consuming. You should have heeded my advice and been patient."*

"Everything will be fine. I have faith in my men."

"I'm sure you do."

I opened my eyes to thin slits in the darkness of my first floor hotel room, trying to hold still and keep my breathing steady and even. In the gray light filtering through the window, I saw the silhouette of a man kneeling below the frame. Another slipped through the open window. Both were as silent as shadows crossing over a gravestone.

The second man entered the room, turned and shut the window behind him. The first man stood and made an obscure gesture with his hands in the direction of my backpack, which sat on a nearby chair, and on noiseless feet, his partner walked toward it.

The first man removed a long, thin-bladed stiletto from a sheath at his waist. He moved toward me.

I remembered Shalizander's words. *"Destroy them!"*

Easy to say, I thought. *For someone who tortures people.*

"Be warned, daughter," Shalizander said. *"These men mean to kill you and take the Boards. Only death will stop them."*

"I don't want to kill anybody," I said. *"There's been more than enough of that in my life already."*

"Sometimes, our choices are limited. Do nothing and die. Destroy them and live."

They're here to kill me and take the Boards! This thought ran through my head in a repeated mantra. I didn't want to kill anybody, but if Shalizander was right, Simon could be in danger, too.

The man with the knife was standing next to the bed, and I could see the gleam of the blade through my slitted eyes. I needed to make a decision, and I needed to do it now. Limited choices, without a doubt, but in the end, I would be the one with more deaths on my conscience.

I reached out with my mind to the Board of the Flames. *"I am the Keeper of the Boards. My will is your will. Hear me and obey!"*

The Board of the Flames spoke in my mind, its voice the roar of a foundry furnace, the sharp crack of a raging forest fire. *"I hear, Keeper. My will is your will. What is your command?"*

I paused for a fraction of a second, even as one of the men reached for my backpack and the other stood over me, preparing to end my life. I had no other choice. I was no match for them physically. My only defense was the Boards. *"Destroy them."*

The Board of the Flames laughed and an image of destruction so vast filled my mind that I gasped aloud.

The man standing above me drew back in surprise. "She's awake!" he hissed.

Before the other man could form a response, he burst into flames so quickly that he didn't even scream. All the oxygen was gone from his lungs, which were seared shut in an instant. The inferno was so hot it looked almost white, and I felt the sudden heat wash over the room like a flood.

The man next to my bed stepped toward his companion, perhaps thinking to help, when he, too, burst into flame. There was an intense *whoosh*, like the furnace in my grandfather's house coming on, only a thousand times louder, and then his body was outlined in fire. Fortunately, the flames were so thick that I didn't see them as they burned, which was just as good—I had enough nightmares to deal with already.

In seconds, both men were piles of ash on the floor. There was nothing else left. Not even their bones or the shining metal blades of their stilettos.

"How delicious," the Board of the Flames said. *"For many years, I received nourishment from the cults that threw their victims into the heart of Mount Vesuvius. For long years after, I took but a small meal from those who used the volcano as a place of cremation. But this . . . ah, this feels much better."*

I shuddered and wondered what exactly the Board meant, but before I could question it further, I heard Simon on the other side of the door. "Jenna!" he called. "Are you all right?"

It was a strangely difficult question to answer, and when I didn't respond, Simon put his shoulder against the door and shoved it open just as I turned on the light. Smoke lingered in the air and the stench of burned flesh filled my nostrils.

"What the—" Simon began, and then stopped when he saw the piles of ash on the floor. "What happened in here?"

"They broke in," I said. "They were going to kill me and take the Boards."

Simon didn't reply for several long moments. Then he nodded, almost to himself. It crossed my mind that perhaps he was praying, though whether for their souls or my forgiveness, I didn't know.

"You had no choice, daughter," Shalizander

whispered in my mind. *"Not about what you made the Board of the Flames do to those men, nor about your destiny."*

Simon was talking. ". . . we need to get out of here, Jenna."

"What?" I asked.

"I said we need to get out of here before the authorities or anyone else comes," he said. "But since these aren't Peraud's men—I can't imagine they'd have regrouped this quickly—that means there's another player."

"And we don't know who," I said, thinking of Peraud strapped down to wooden planks and being tortured by Shalizander. No, it certainly wasn't Peraud. That much, at least, was certain.

"Perhaps," he said. "But I can make a guess."

"Who?"

"Later," he said. "Right now, we've got to move."

The smoke had dissipated, but I suspected the smell would be very difficult, if not impossible, to get out of the room. What cleaning product could there possibly be to remove the scent of charred human flesh and bones from carpeting and curtains?

"Get your things together," Simon said. "We'll leave as soon as you're ready."

Simon slipped out as I climbed out of bed, stepping carefully to avoid the ash piles, and dressed. I hadn't unpacked before going to bed, so it only took a minute to toss a few things into my duffel bag.

Simon came back carrying his bag and hefted mine as well. I pulled on my leather jacket and picked up my backpack.

"Are we going to check out?" I asked, as we walked down the hallway.

"No," he said shortly. "Let's hope the authorities file it as an unsolved mystery. It didn't look like there was very much left."

"Not even a trace of bone, Keeper," the Board of the Flames said, still gloating about its recent meal.

"There wasn't," I said.

Simon and I stepped into the misty pre-dawn, and walked several blocks before he called a halt next to a bench. "This will do," he said, putting down the bags and sitting.

"For what?" I asked. "Where are we going anyway?"

"For me to get myself together," Simon said. "You just burned two men alive, Jenna! And you don't seem to feel much of anything about it."

Feeling defensive, I said, "What do you want me to feel about it? They were going to kill me!"

"Ever heard of minimum necessary force?" Simon snapped. "A little restraint, maybe?"

"Restraint?" I half-shouted. "For what? So they could come back and try again? Why do you think we had so many problems with Peraud?"

Rising back to his feet, Simon's blue eyes captured mine. From between clenched teeth, he said, "So we could *question* them, Jenna. We might have gotten some useful information out of them."

Deflated, I said, "Well, they didn't seem all that interested in talking to me."

For a moment, Simon stared at me. "All right," he said. "I'm sorry. It's just not like you to harm someone like that. I was caught off-guard."

"*You* were caught off-guard?" I said. "It didn't seem like I had much of a choice."

He put a comforting hand on my shoulder. "I don't think you did," he said. "Let's figure out where we go from here."

"How do we do that?" I asked. "Whoever those men were, they didn't have any trouble finding us."

"So we'll cover our tracks better this time."

"How?" I asked.

He removed his cell phone from his pocket and quickly dialed a number. "That's what we have Armand for," he said. "He can help us disappear."

I nodded, but my mind had already moved on to something else entirely. If those men had found us within a day of arriving in Scotland, they hadn't been sent.

We'd been followed.

The wolves from the tunnels were loose, and there was no doubt in my mind that I was being hunted. The only questions were by whom and when would they catch up to me?

"Armand agrees that we were followed out of Rome," Simon confirmed over breakfast later that morning. We'd found another hotel, stored our luggage in the rental car, and decided to take the time to eat before we left. "So, we're going to the Highlands in a different car, plus he's going to make it look like we flew to several different destinations from Edinburgh today."

"That's clever," I said, taking a bite of toast. "But I don't think it will work."

"Why not?" he asked.

"Just a feeling," I said, thinking again of the human wolves of my dream and the relentless way they had hunted me.

"Well, it's worth a try."

The desk manager of the hotel we had found stopped by our table with a package. "This just arrived for you, sir," he said to Simon.

"Thank you," Simon said, taking the bulky envelope. "Armand was able to contact the messenger after all," he said. "He said he'd shipped this to us yesterday, and wasn't sure if he'd catch them in time to keep us from having to go back to the hotel."

"What is it?" I asked.

Simon ripped open the package and removed a large, heavy book that looked very old. "*The True Story of Myrddin, Laird of Scotland.*"

"Remember what I said about searching for clues in a mall or a coffee shop?" I asked. "Why is it always old, musty books?"

Simon smiled and opened the front cover. A note on plain white paper fell out, and I saw Armand's signature below the crisp, neat handwriting. "What does it say?"

He looked it over briefly. "Armand says that it isn't known for certain where Arthur fought his last battle—with Merlin's help—but the most likely place to find Camallan is somewhere in the Ochil Hills region."

"I'm guessing there isn't a mall within a hundred miles," I said.

"Probably not," Simon admitted. "Have you been able to hear the Board of the Earth yet?"

I shook my head, remembering my aborted attempts from earlier. "No. The others are too noisy. Every time I even think to try, they start talking to me. Maybe they'll let me do it later."

His fork halfway to his mouth, Simon paused and said, "*Let* you?"

"That's not what I meant," I objected, but my thoughts were otherwise. That *is* what I had meant.

"Keeper, remember that we have warned you in the past about Simon and Armand," the Board of the Winds said. *"They fear your growing powers and seek to keep you under their control."*

"As do you," I said.

"No," the Board of the Waters chimed in. *"Our will is your will. But you must be educated in the proper time. Too much too quickly and you will fail as surely as if you had not tried at all."*

"Jenna!" Simon snapped, and my attention went back to him.

"What?" I asked.

"I was talking to you," Simon said. "You seem very distracted these days."

"You would be, too," I said. "I'm having multiple conversations at once, remember?"

"Dario taught you how to quiet them," he said.

"It . . . doesn't always work," I admitted. "But let's get back to the matter at hand. When are we leaving?"

Simon looked like he wanted to say more, and his gaze was full of unspoken questions, but instead he said, "As soon as we finish breakfast. If I can't make sure you sleep, at least I can try to make sure you're fed."

I placed my napkin on the plate. "Nice try, but I'm finished. Let's get going."

He took a final sip of coffee and got to his feet. "Okay, Jenna. No time like the present, eh?"

"Something like that." But the truth was that I was filled with nervous energy. I wanted to get moving, keep moving. I could almost feel the wolves closing in on us.

And the sooner I got to the phoenix stone, the sooner I could get to the fourth Board and blessed relief from all the voices echoing in my head.

Simon drove our new rental into the rolling hills of Scotland. Even though it was early spring, the grass was already a deep, healthy green and growing rapidly. From time to time, he consulted a small map book on the dashboard. Eventually, he said, "We're nearing Falkirk, and should be entering the Ochil Hills region now."

He had been quiet during the drive, but I didn't have a lot to say myself. Over and over I replayed the vision I'd experienced in the Tower with Shalizander and Peraud. What were the limits to her powers, if any? And had I heard, or just imagined the tiny note of fear in her voice when she spoke of Malkander? These were the questions I focused on, but when Simon spoke, I turned my attention back to what we were doing.

Staring at the landscape, an idea came to me, and I focused my will on the Boards. *"Do you know of this place we seek? Do you know where Camallan is?"*

The Board of the Flames replied first, its snapping voice heavy with disdain. *"That is a name that has not been forgotten by the elements of this place, Keeper."*

"Can you help me find it?" I pressed.

"Within the pages of the book sent to you by Armand is a map. You paged past it at the restaurant earlier, so I know it's there. Turn to it again, so that I may see it in your mind."

I did as the Board asked, paging through the book until I came to a map marked with ancient symbols and barely legible text. *"So?"* I asked.

"We should be able to assist you, yes," it replied. Its voice sounded almost reluctant. I considered asking more questions, but given how much pressure

the Boards were already placing on me, decided against it.

The hills around us were studded with ancient cairn stones, placed there to mark a burial site or a battle or other event, and the road was little more than a dirt track that had been paved over at one point in time, but never maintained. There was very little traffic in the area, as it didn't seem to be a likely spot for tourism.

I heard the Boards in my head, talking back and forth to one another, but what they were saying was beyond me. Simon pulled the car over to the side of the road.

"Why are we stopping?" I asked.

"I thought we might get out and take a look around," he said. "There's a lot of cairns out there, and maybe one of them will give us a clue."

"It doesn't look right," I said.

"What do you mean?"

"In my dream, with Merlin, there were trees. A lot of trees."

Simon thought about it for a minute, and then shrugged. "That was a long time ago, Jenna. I'm not very knowledgeable about this part of the world, but they could have died out or been chopped down centuries ago."

"Or they could have been a part of the dream itself, put there by Merlin." I looked out at the hills and the stones. "Let's go, then. I wouldn't mind stretching my legs anyway."

We wandered over the landscape, looking at ancient cairns and random piles of stones for almost an hour. The whole time, I heard the Boards conferring in my mind, and could barely focus on where I was putting my feet, let alone anything Simon might have been saying.

Finally, I couldn't take it anymore.

"Vixistbra!" I practically screamed at them. The sudden silence was almost noisier than they had been. "For goodness sake, shut up and help me!"

When none of them responded, I grudgingly said, *"Grametex."* The word in the Language of the Birds that meant "speak."

"Many of these stones bear ancient sigils, Keeper," the Board of the Waters said. *"Runes that correspond to the various elements."*

"Fire, water, air, and earth are all represented in places," the Board of the Winds added.

"Simon wait," I said aloud. "I need to think."

He moved back to me and remained silent, watching as I communicated with the Boards.

"Look, I've just about had it up to here with your whispering nonsense. Now answer my questions. Am I in the right area to find the location of Camallan?" I asked.

"Yes," the Board of the Winds replied. *"It was near here that Merlin fought at Arthur's side during his final battle against the Picts."*

Thinking rapidly, I said, *"So which stone is the right one?"*

"There is only one right one, Keeper," the Board of the Flames said. *"As there is only one correct question."*

They loved to play word games, it seemed. Or perhaps something in their very nature prevented them from answering anything but a particular question. *Or maybe this was why all the previous Keepers died,* I thought. *They were all driven insane by these Boards' stupid riddles.*

Thinking of the phoenix, I played a hunch. *"Which stone most strongly combines the elements of fire and air?"*

There was a sudden surge of laughter in my head, and a sense of pleasure.

"Well done, Keeper," the Board of the Waters said. *"She grows more astute with each passing day, my brothers."*

"And more powerful," the Board of the Flames said.

"Just answer me," I demanded.

"You have asked the proper question, so you shall have a proper answer," it said. *"Walk north twenty paces."*

I waved for Simon to follow, and the Board of the Flames led me over the ground, giving me directions and leading me over a brief series of hills until we reached a set of stones that I recognized immediately.

"That's it!" I said. From where we were walking, the marker hadn't been visible.

Sitting atop a square-shaped marker was the

phoenix stone. The symbols on the marker itself were unfamiliar, but the symbols on the phoenix stone itself—even though it was small and weathered—were just as they had been in my dream with Merlin.

"We've found it." I reached out to take it off the marker.

Simon threw out his hand to stop me as he said, "Jenna, wait!"

But it was too late.

The trap had already been sprung.

At the base of the stone marker, a shadowy form began to appear, seeming to flow up from the ground. Simon and I stepped backward, and the hair on the back of my neck rose as a chill slid down my spine.

The form grew more solid and I recognized the man from my dream with Emrys. Although I could still see through him, he seemed more substantial than the spirits I had dealt with in Pompeii.

"That's the other wizard, Coghlan," I muttered to Simon. "He fought Merlin in my dream."

"I remember you mentioning him," Simon said.

I already knew from hard experience that the powers of the Boards could not affect a spirit; they were immune to the elements. I had learned that in Pompeii, when the angry spirits of the dead there nearly took my life with their freezing touch. "Ideas?" I asked Simon.

At that moment, Coghlan muttered an incantation, and the phoenix stone leaped out of my hands and into his. He cradled it carefully, before slipping it into a pocket of his robes.

His voice sounded as real as Simon's. "I knew that eventually someone would come here, seeking the phoenix stone."

"You were banished by the wizard Emrys," Simon said. "Why haven't you moved on to the next world?"

"I am the Keeper of the Boards," I called. *"Your will is my will."*

The Board of the Winds answered. *"What is your will, Keeper?"*

"I need a gale. Let us blow this spirit into the next world."

"I was waiting," Coghlan replied, his voice calm and steady. "Waiting for my opportunity to grasp the Emrys's power for my own."

"You know this will not work, Keeper," it replied.

"Do it!" I demanded.

When I had first begun using the Board of Air, summoning wind took time. Now it appeared in an instant, a solid wall of invisible energy that flattened the grass and even shook the stones. I felt it pass and watched as it slammed into Coghlan's insubstantial form. He immediately dissipated, but as the wind passed, he reformed again.

"I am not subject to the powers you wield, Keeper," Coghlan said. "The elements of this world cannot harm me."

"That's what all you spirits say," I replied.

"Bring me a storm," I said to the Board of the Waters.

In moments, clouds boiled overhead, black and heavy.

"Wind and rain!" I cried. The sky opened and buckets of rain slashed down, turning to ice pellets. The Board of the Winds caused another gale-force wind to swirl past the area. As before, Coghlan's form dispersed as the elements struck him, only to knit back together as they passed.

"Burn him!" I called out to the Board of the Flames.

A familiar *whoosh* echoed over the hills and the flames appeared to consume Coghlan, then flickered and died away.

"There is nothing to burn, Keeper," the Board of the Flames said. *"He is not of this world."*

"Damn it!" I cried.

"Jenna," Simon said, his voice sounding calm. "That's enough. We can't beat him this way."

"I am the Keeper of the Boards," I screamed. "I. Want. That. Stone!"

I could hear the sound of Shalizander's voice in my own, her rage in my mind, but I ignored it. I had to have the stone or there would be no peace for me.

I called on the Boards once more, demanding that they respond. Sheets of icy rain, winds that knocked down stones that had stood for several hundred years, bursts of fire that would incinerate steel swept through the spirit of Coghlan—and all of them failed.

Exhausted and trembling, I relaxed my will.

"I sense your surrender, Keeper," Coghlan said, laughing, mocking me. "Though your powers are formidable, they are ineffective where I am concerned. Now, you will lead me to the Emrys's final resting place, and the Board of the Earth—along with the others that you carry—will at last be mine."

He sounded so calm and so certain, that I knew he was right. Though I hated to admit it, there was little else I could do except play along and hope to somehow get the phoenix stone back from him before we figured out where Merlin's tomb was located. If we could.

I began to speak, but Simon put a restraining hand on my shoulder. "Let me try."

He stepped forward. I wanted to stop him, I didn't want to see him get hurt, but there was something in the way he moved, the calm in his voice, that bade me keep silent.

He walked in front of me, closing the distance between Coghlan and himself.

And though it was barely visible, I saw that his body was outlined in a faint, white light.

Whatever spirit had possessed him in Miller's Crossing, that had allowed him to snatch Tom from death's door, was back. I hadn't been a practicing Catholic in a long time. Not really. But a small voice inside—not the Boards or Shalizander—said that what I was seeing at that moment was a sign of true faith, and of God's enduring power to those who believed.

A sense of peace washed over me, and I wondered at the sudden quiet of the Boards.

But then I saw Coghlan's eyes widen and the first words of a spell leave his lips. Simon wouldn't stand a chance.

This was a fight of magic, not faith, and Simon wasn't suited for the battle at all.

"My men were killed—utterly destroyed!"

"I urged patience, but you refused to heed me. These artifacts are like no other you have ever dealt with, and young Jenna Solitaire is much more than she appears to be."

"I should have listened to you. I couldn't imagine her having such powers. What should I do now?"

"Send more men. They will probably go to ground and soon, if for no other reason than I am not convinced they know where the Board of the Earth is located."

"Where will they go?"

"To a friend and a location they believe to be safe. Send your men to England. They can pick up the trail again at Armand's estate."

Simon must have sensed my doubt, because he paused and looked back at me. In that same calm voice, he said, "Jenna, there are some battles that must be fought with faith, not magic."

Trying to keep the desperation out of my voice, I said, "Simon, this *is* a battle with magic."

He smiled once more and said, "Watch and be restored."

Before I could ask what he meant, he turned back to the spirit.

Coghlan finished muttering his incantation, and I heard the force in his final words. He pointed his staff at Simon and then . . . nothing. Nothing happened at all. He quickly said the words again, and once more pointed at Simon. With the exact same result.

Stunned, Coghlan shook his head. "How—how could this be?"

"You have remained here for a long time," Simon said. "It is only your will that holds your soul to the earth, not your body or your mind. Those have long since decayed into dust."

"I am Coghlan!" the sorcerer shrieked. "I will be the master of the earth!"

Simon smiled sadly. "Even if she were to agree to lead you to Emrys's tomb, you cannot leave this place, Coghlan. Your spirit is trapped here by your hatred and anger, not your magic. Your magic died long ago."

"No!" Coghlan screamed again. He removed a wand from the folds of his robes and pointed it, muttering harsh words of power. As with his own spells, this one also failed.

"All that holds you here is the power of your

belief," Simon said. "It's time to move on, to let go. You will be forgiven."

"Who are you to forgive me?" Coghlan said.

"Your forgiveness does not come from me, Coghlan."

"Then who?"

Simon reached into his jacket and removed a small, stoppered ceramic bottle. "The Lord God," he said. He took the top off the bottle and stepped forward. "For too long have you lingered here, Coghlan."

"No!" Coghlan screamed, shuddering as he tried to flee, but unable to go anywhere. "The One God has no power over me! I must have the Boards! I am immortal!"

Simon poured a droplet out of the bottle and I saw oil glistening on his fingertips. "I'm sorry, Coghlan, but the One God has power over all. He always has. You are not an immortal. You are not even a pure spirit, simply a soul that has gone unreleased by time. Your hatred and desire have kept you here long after you should have faced judgment."

Coghlan gibbered and screeched, writhing and twisting like a sheet on a clothesline in a high wind.

Simon reached out and swiped the oil across Coghlan's forehead. For a moment, it hung in the air, and then disappeared. "Through this holy anointing may the Lord in his love and mercy help you with the grace of the Holy Spirit. May the Lord who frees you from sin save you and raise you up."

I heard an odd ripping sound, and then Coghlan's

form rose away from the stone marker, dissipating with each passing second. "I will return!" he cried. "I will not be defeated!"

Simon made the sign of the cross and said, "Godspeed, Coghlan, and may your judgment be swift and merciful."

Coghlan tried to say more, stretching out with his now-ghostly arms to grasp the stone marker. The phoenix stone slipped through his insubstantial fingers and dropped to the ground.

"Retrieve the stone, daughter!" Shalizander cried in my head. *"It's more powerful than you know."*

"Pick up the phoenix stone, Keeper. That is the pathway to our brother!" the Boards called.

The last remnants of Coghlan's soul disappeared as Simon bent down to pick up the phoenix stone. "That was fascinating. I've heard of such occurrences happening, but have never witnessed it myself."

In my mind's eye, I saw the Tower once more, with Shalizander standing at the window. Behind her, I heard even Peraud cry at me to pick up the stone.

"Daughter, heed me!" Shalizander said.

With my physical eyes, I watched Simon bend down and grasp the stone. While in my mind, I saw and heard Shalizander, the Boards, and Peraud all telling me to pick it up, pick it up, *pick it up right now!*

Simon rose from his crouch, holding the phoenix stone in his hands. He turned to me.

"You fool," Shalizander said. *"The phoenix stone is no mere trinket. It's a powerful artifact!"*

"I'll get it," I snapped.

"Give it to me!" she shrieked, and then I felt her within me, a part of me. Every inch of my body itched horribly and I felt like I was bending in different, impossible directions.

She was *inside* me, and before I could think of what to do or say or how to respond, I heard my voice say without my control, "Give it to me!"

I felt myself lurch forward, my hands outstretched for the stone, even as Simon backed away in utter confusion.

In my mind, Shalizander said, *"I am the Creator of the Boards. Hear me and obey!"*

The Board of the Winds responded immediately. *"We hear and obey, Mistress."*

"Take it from him!" she called.

A sudden flare of power and a massive wall of wind swirled around us.

I gathered my will, feeling Shalizander's presence as an almost physical thing inside me.

"Get out of my mind!" I screamed at her, pushing with all my mental strength. *"Get out!"*

I watched, apart from myself, as the winds reached out and picked Simon up as though he were a rag doll.

"Leave him alone," I ordered the Board of the Winds. *"Stop right now!"*

"Jenna, what are you doing? What's wrong?" Simon called.

"You are the Keeper, but Shalizander is the Creator. We are bound to her will even more tightly than we are bound to yours," it responded.

The winds grew stronger, and Simon was now ten feet off the ground, clutching the stone to his chest. He didn't cry out, but simply tried to hang on.

"Now!" Shalizander ordered.

And the winds suddenly reversed course and threw Simon to the ground. He landed with the heavy thud of a grain sack, slamming into the moist earth with such force that he actually bounced.

The phoenix stone tumbled out of his hands and I felt my body move to pick it up.

I had to fight her. In her madness, she had grown to be as evil as the Boards themselves. Perhaps she always had been.

"No!" I said, gritting my teeth and shoving against Shalizander's presence in my mind. *"Get out!"*

"Daughter, why must you fight me so?" Shalizander asked, holding her ground. But I could hear the strain in her voice as she added, *"I seek only to protect you, to ensure that your destiny is fulfilled."*

"Because you didn't ask!" I snarled, shoving harder.

I pictured her back in her Tower, and the scene shifted. At the same time, I called to Simon, trying to rouse him from where he lay stunned.

We were back in Shalizander's room in the Tower. Peraud was still chained to the wooden beams, his eyes wide as we appeared out of nowhere, our hands clasped against each other, shoving back and forth like two dogs fighting over a bone.

"I won't let you control me like this," I said, shoving harder. *"It's* my *life.* My *choice."*

Breathing heavily, Shalizander said, *"In this, daughter, you have no choice."*

In the real world, I kept calling Simon's name, and then he was there. I felt him standing next to me, a little dazed but very much alive.

"Jenna," he said. "Take my hand."

"We're not finished yet," Shalizander said. *"You need to decide what's more important to you—finding all of the Boards and defeating Malkander, or doing things your way and risking everything."*

I reached out and felt Simon's hand grip mine. It was warm and calloused and very real. His deep voice sounded calm as he said, "Jenna, it's all right. I'm here. Come back to me."

"Shalizander speaks the truth, Keeper," Peraud called out. *"Malkander's powers are vast. To defeat him, you will need all your allies."* He put a strange stress on the word "allies," and I wondered what he truly meant.

I looked at them both and shook my head. *"Allies, yes. Surrender my soul? Never."*

I closed my eyes and focused all my will on Simon.

I felt myself move away from the Tower, and ignored Shalizander's demands to come back. She acted like she was my mother, but in truth she meant nothing to me. She was just one more burden to deal with. She was not trustworthy—not any more so than Peraud or even Malkander. Though it appeared that in his desperation, Peraud now wanted to switch sides. I didn't blame him.

"Jenna," Simon said. "Open your eyes."

I did and he was right there in front of me. The one man in this world that I *knew* I could trust and count on. His coat was spattered with wet grass and mud, but he was very much real and I didn't hesitate. I threw myself into his arms and sobbed like a child.

We stood that way, holding each other, for a long time. He didn't say anything, just stroked my hair and held me until I finally quieted. Then he led me over to the stone marker and helped me sit nearby.

"This is called a Pict stone," he said quietly, touching the marker. "It's been here for a long, long time. They used them to commemorate important battles."

I sniffled, and dug through my backpack to find something resembling a tissue.

"Every single person in this world fights battles, Jenna," he continued. "Some are easy, some are hard. We win some and we lose some. Sometimes, we even lose people close to us—those who choose to fight at our side or somehow get caught up in the battle by accident.

"What matters, I have come to believe, is that we face our life with the knowledge that our friends and family and God are all rooting for us to succeed—not in terms of winning or losing, but in terms of life. Those who love us want to see us happy. I want to see you happy, too, Jenna." He turned away from the marker and stared at me, once more capturing my eyes with his. "More than anything else, I wish you'd tell me what's really going on."

I finished composing myself and sighed. "I'm not sure where to begin."

Simon sat down next to me. "Whereever it feels right," he said. "Just talk."

So I did. Slowly at first, my voice cracked and tired, but soon the words poured out. There was a sense of relief in telling it all to him, in sharing the burdens I carried just a little bit. I explained about the ritual of the dagger and how Shalizander had been pushing me to complete it for days. I told him how the Boards and Shalizander were talking to me constantly and how—even dead—she seemed to have so much power over them and me. The only thing I didn't mention was Peraud. There was no point in causing Simon pain by telling him that his brother was spending his afterlife being tortured.

It felt incredibly good to talk about what had been happening, if for no other reason than to share it. I'm not sure a burden shared is a burden halved, but it did feel better to talk about it instead of just sitting in the dark, hoping everything would somehow get better by itself.

Finally, I said, "What it comes down to is that she wants to possess me, because she believes that's the only way I'll be able to fight Malkander and win. She almost had me this time, and I didn't even complete the ritual."

"What do *you* believe, Jenna?" Simon asked. "That's the important thing, you know. Your belief and faith in yourself and God."

"I don't know *what* to believe," I admitted. "I saw you bring my best friend practically back from the dead and send a man's soul on its way to heaven, but that still doesn't mean God makes a lot of sense to me. Where was he when *I* needed him? Where was he when my parents were killed?"

Simon smiled, and then handed me the phoenix stone. "Put this in your pack, where it will be safe."

I put the stone—it was only a small cube, and it easily fit into an outer pocket—away, while I waited for Simon's answer.

After a time, he said, "As a priest, I've heard that question a lot. Where was God when this bad thing or that bad thing was happening? It's ironic, in a way, because the people asking that are still here. They're still alive, and living and loving and doing all the things that are truly important in life."

"So you're saying an absentee God is better than none at all?"

He laughed and shook his head. "No, what I'm saying is that God is right where he's supposed to be. He protects us when he should, and leaves us to our own devices when it's critical that we learn something—even if it's something hard to bear. God never challenges us with a mountain we cannot climb."

"Malkander might be tougher than any mountain," I said. "Maybe the bottom line, Simon, is that I'm scared. Terrified to do something wrong, or to lose control of the Boards. I don't trust Shalizander and I don't trust the Boards. What if they fall into the wrong hands or, worse still, I lose control of them like I did the first time, and they completely destroy a city? Or kill hundreds—or thousands of innocent people? I don't know how I would handle that."

He guided me to my feet and we began walking back toward the car. "You may have trouble accepting this," he said, "but I believe in you."

I stopped and looked at him closely. "Why?"

"Because these things just have a way of working themselves out for the good," he replied. "I have faith that no matter what a given prophecy says, or what challenges we face, God will choose the right person for the right job. For this, he chose you. I know you'll do the right things, Jenna, because that's how God made you."

We walked in silence for a time as I thought about that. "Do you think I should complete the ritual?" I asked as we reached the car.

He opened my door for me. "No," he said. "Not ever, if it can be helped, and at the least, not yet."

"Why?"

"Because you're stronger than Shalizander or the Boards give you credit for. It may come to that if Malkander is as powerful as she claims, but right now, he's not our problem. We haven't seen any sign of him since we left Pompeii." He walked around to the driver's side and got in.

"So what's our problem?" I asked.

"Lunch," he said, starting the engine. "I'm starved."

"Lunch?" I asked, incredulous. "How can you be hungry at a time like this?"

"You've got to eat to survive," he said. "Besides, that was a lot of work back there." He turned in his seat to face me, and his tone went serious. "Jenna, you must have faith in yourself. There may come a point when you need Shalizander's aid, but we haven't reached it yet."

I didn't say anything as I thought about his words, and then I nodded. "Thank you. For everything."

Looking at him, I felt my heart contract painfully. I knew what *could* have been between us, just as I knew that all the "could-have-been's" in the world wouldn't change what was necessary for us to complete my quest.

"That's what friends are for," he said.

He started the engine and turned the car around, heading for the nearby village of Blackford. The next day, we'd be heading to London. We drove in companionable silence, thinking our own thoughts—mine were mainly about how happy I was that the Boards and Shalizander were both quiet for now—when something else occurred to me.

When Simon had healed Tom in the hospital back in Miller's Crossing, he'd claimed to have no memory of anything special at all.

This time, when I'd mentioned that and what I'd seen him do with Coghlan's spirit, he hadn't said a single word of denial. He had remembered.

Maybe, like me, there were some things that he just didn't want to talk about.

Later that evening, after we'd checked into our lodgings in Blackford and eaten a good, hearty meal of stewed lamb, with potatoes, carrots, and homemade bread—my appetite had returned with a vengeance after our conversation—I locked myself into my room, and double-checked that the windows were locked tight.

I luxuriated in a bath for a while and combed out my hair, which was still in desperate need of a trim, then curled up on the bed and pulled the BlackBerry out. The clerk at the desk said that their Internet service wasn't the most reliable—it tended to go off and on during windy days—but I held out hope that I'd be able to check e-mail.

I took me two tries, but I managed to get a connection and saw that there was a message from Tom. I opened it and read:

J.—

I'm sorry to have worried you. I'm okay, I promise.

I can't tell you where I am right now, but I'll be in touch as soon as possible. I think Kristen is in some real trouble. I don't know what's happened to her, but she's not the same person you or I knew just a short time ago.

Be safe, and I'll be in touch soon.

Your friend,

Tom

Troubled, I drafted a quick reply, hoping he'd read it soon.

Dear Tom—

I don't know what's going on, but please consider telling me where you are and what's going on. Maybe I can help, maybe not, but . . .

I stopped typing for a moment, remembering what Simon had said earlier, and it brought a smile to my face. I continued typing.

. . . that's what friends are for. And I am your friend.

Take care of yourself and please get in touch soon.

Always,

Jenna

I checked my other messages, then signed off, glad that the connection held. I exchanged the BlackBerry for the Chronicle, yet another source of worry and consternation.

Reading it usually made me sick—sometimes horribly sick—but I needed information. The Chronicle was the best source of information for how other Keepers had dealt with the Boards, as each of them had entered her story into its magical pages. Shalizander's daughter, Malizander, had almost certainly faced the same problem I had. I knew she resisted completing the ritual, but eventually she'd done it.

But I had other questions that needed answering. What had driven her to that point? Had Shalizander truly shared Malizander's body and mind, or had it been a form of possession, leaving the real Malizander trapped somewhere inside herself, screaming for release? If not, what did happen and how did she deal with it?

I opened the cover of the Chronicle and began paging through it. "Talk to me, Malizander. Before it's too late."

I barely let my eyes touch a passage, skimming

words and moving on before they'd completely registered. It was, I thought, a bit like channel-surfing.

Finally, there was a notation that caught my eye. It read:

To the Daughter of Destiny,

A warning . . .

And I fell, tumbling, into a vision, and a message that had been waiting for me for over a thousand years.

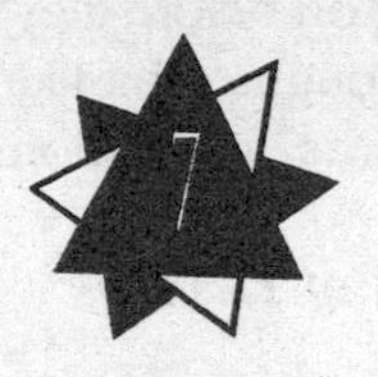

"They haven't been seen at Armand's estate. Are you sure that's where they'll go?"

"I'm certain of it. Keep your men in position and tell them to wait. They should only observe her."

"Why? Shouldn't we attempt to apprehend her when she shows up? I have ways of ensuring that she'll tell us everything we need to know about the Board of the Earth."

"Such crude measures ensure nothing. If you are patient, she will take you to the Board with no coercion required on your part at all."

Malizander's eyes are the green of uncut emeralds and her hair is such a dark shade of red that it's almost black. She smiles, and I know that this vision is unlike any other I have had. It feels different, more of an experience to participate in than a ride to simply hang on to.

"You're the one," she says. "The Daughter of Destiny."

"Yes," I say. "I am." I look around and see a room not all that different from the one in Shalizander's Tower. "This looks familiar to me."

"It should," she says, "this is the same room that you see in Shalizander's sendings. I created this . . . vision, if you will . . . from there. Not long before the Tower itself disappeared for the last time."

"What . . . ?"

"Is all this?" she finishes my question. Her laughter is light, like a melody. "This is a sending vision. I sent it to you long ago, so that when the prophecy was finally being fulfilled, I could offer some small amount of aid."

"And when it's over?"

"The last traces of Malizander—me—will be gone," she says. "Even the page you read within the Chronicle will cease to exist."

Sensing that time is of the essence, I say, "What can you tell me?"

"More, I think, than you want to know," she says. "Once, I was like you are now. Alive to the possibilities of the world. That all ended when the Boards were created. The last true bastion of magical learning came to an end with the fall of the Tower and the death of so many of our kind."

"Our kind?"

"Those who use magic," she said. "During the height of our power, we served as advisors to kings and emperors, worked amazing spells that shook the very foundations of the world. Some of us even were kings. But the fall of the Tower, with its strong

connections to the magical forces of the world, destroyed many of us."

She walks closer and peers carefully at me. "You are not a spell caster, are you?"

I shake my head.

"Then you face a hard road," she says. "Had my circumstances been even a little different, I might have been an even greater sorceress than my mother. As it was, when she pressed me to do the ritual and I agreed . . . my life was no longer my own."

"How is it that she still lives, while you are . . ."

"Dead?" Malizander smiles. "The magic of the dagger. It is tied to the essence of Shalizander—her soul—and no other's. While it preserves her within the magical sanctuary she had created, it cannot do the same for anyone else."

"And Peraud?"

"I can see who he is in your mind. His body was destroyed by my father, Malkander, leaving his spirit trapped in Shalizander's control. I hold few doubts that he knew this. Should he have desired, he could have preserved Peraud's body and brought his soul back. He would have died a normal death and gone on to the next world."

"So if I complete the ritual, what will happen?"

"You will be faced with a very difficult choice, but not an impossible one. Shalizander will want complete control of your mind and your body. Should you allow this, you will no longer be yourself, but a host for Shalizander's spirit. The Boards

will respond to her, rather than you, and any decisions you make will be determined by her."

"That's a cheery thought," I say. "What's the good news?"

"The good news is that you can fight. In her current state, Shalizander is powerful, yes, but not all powerful. Your will must be stronger than her will. It is not a battle of magics, but a battle of personalities." Malizander turns away and looks out the window. "I had forgotten how beautiful they were."

I walk behind her and look out the window. Unlike Shalizander's view, this one is of the hanging gardens, the sun kissing leaves of green plants and blooming flowers. It is breathtaking. "You're not telling me something," I say.

"Any battle you win over her will be brief victory at best. She will never rest, nor stop seeking a way to bend you to her wishes."

"How did you survive the ritual, then?" I press. "I know you did. I found your warning stone near Pompeii."

She turns to me and leans on the window frame. "I didn't survive. Not truly. I spent most of my days as a slave to her will. I was only able to take control of my mind and body for brief periods."

"For the rest of your life?" I ask, aghast at the notion.

"Yes," she says. "In the end, I was finally able to reclaim control long enough to complete this spell, and then I destroyed myself. As I had hoped, the

magical framework of the Chronicle preserved my magic long enough for us to speak."

"What are my choices, then?" I ask. "I'm not a sorceress! I'm an ordinary teenager in over her head. Way over. How can I beat Malkander without her aid?"

A sadness appears in her eyes. "I do not believe you can. And there is little I can do to help you. Once this vision is complete, Shalizander will have total control over the Chronicle and the Tower. Even now, she senses that we are conversing and is seeking to bring an end to the spell."

I wonder how to ask my next question, but she beats me to it.

"Harbor no doubts that where Shalizander is concerned, her obsession with the Boards has consumed her. She is powerful, yes, but she is also mad. And with madness comes unreason and chaos. Perhaps the Boards themselves did this to her. Perhaps all the long years of frustration and imprisonment. I do not know for sure, but I do know that you must never trust her."

"I don't," I say. "There is one thing you can tell me."

"Quickly," Malizander says. "Time grows short."

"The prophecy," I say. "I want . . . I need to know what it says."

Malizander nods. "These are the words of Shalizander's prophecy," she says, and recites the verses.

The words burn in my mind and I know I shall never forget them.

"Light moves through arcs of Shadow, Shadows move through arcs of Light,

Good and Evil twist and turn, Noon the same as Night.

The opening of an ancient Gate, the passage into Hell,

Unfold when the Line has Ended, called forth by Faith and Spell.

The last shall be the Champion, to Open and Close the Way,

A final Daughter issued, to bring the Light back to the Day.

Of strong Will and Destiny, this last Keeper of the Boards,

To master One and All, and find the magic Wards.

That protects the hidden Boundary, buried deep beneath the Land,

And stand before the Gates of Hell, bar the Way and make a Stand.

Should this Daughter falter, or fail in her appointed tasks,

Then the Gate shall open forever, and Evil consume the land Unmasked.

Hearken to the Light, my daughters, and watch close the Shadows fall,

All Paths have two directions, but the Boards have none at all."

"Well, that's no help," I say. "No help at all. It leaves more questions than answers."

"Such is the nature of prophecy, and there is little else I can tell you," Malizander says. "But I would remind you that there are two prophecies, and the other is Malkander's. I would also tell you that he is more than an immortal sorcerer—he, as you know, is the father of Simon and Peraud, and countless other male children that have had strong magical abilities through the ages. It is likely that Merlin Emrys was one of them, and that he turned against Malkander, just as Peraud did in Mount Vesuvius."

"Are you saying there could be others out there?" I ask.

She nods. "That is precisely what I am saying."

"Perfect," I say. "I have far more enemies than allies, and even those who should be my allies I cannot trust."

"You can trust yourself," Malizander says. "That's all any of us could ever do. Even in her madness, my mother is trapped by the prophecy and must see it to its end. Only then will she be free."

Suddenly, the image of the Tower room and Malizander wavers in and out of focus.

"We are out of time, Jenna Solitaire," she says. "Shalizander has found a way to disrupt this magic."

"Wait! I have so many other questions!"

"And you will find the answers you need, Daughter of Destiny—if your will remains strong."

"But should I complete the ritual?" I ask, even as she fades.

Her voice is a fleeting whisper. "Only if you

must and are in great need of her magic. And then be ready to battle for your very soul. Fare well, Jenna."

The vision fades, fades and . . .

I woke in my room, shivering and cold. The Chronicle lay next to me, its cover closed. I stared into the darkness, anticipating that Shalizander would say something, but both she and the Boards were silent.

I waited, afraid of her response, until I drifted into a dreamless sleep.

The next morning, Simon and I ate breakfast while I told him about my vision and Malizander. As before, it felt better to talk about it than to keep it to myself. When I mentioned that I had the words to the prophecy, he stopped eating and began taking notes.

"There's a lot there to consider," he said. "This is saying that you will open—and close—the way—*if* you are successful."

"I thought opening the way was a bad thing."

"So did I," he said thoughtfully. "Perhaps we should have Armand look at this. He likes this sort of thing, while my strengths lie elsewhere."

"I'll be interested in hearing what he makes of it," I said, between bites of egg and sausage in a roll. "It doesn't seem all that helpful to me."

"Prophecy tends to be inexact at the best of

times, and is best read in hindsight. That's when it will make sense."

"Marvelous," I said. "What do you make of Malizander's advice about the dagger?"

"I think you should do as she suggests. Just leave it alone. Right now, you have allies, even if we're not all-powerful wizards." He took a sip of his coffee and frowned. It was weaker than either of us preferred.

"That's okay," I said. "There are more than enough all-powerful wizards in my life as it is. I'm perfectly happy to have all of you the way you are."

"That's good," Simon replied. "I don't anticipate taking up the wizard's life anytime soon. It conflicts with my priestly duties." He looked like he was going to say more, but his cell phone rang.

I saw him glance at the screen, and then he answered, "Simon Monk."

He listened to the other caller, and his eyes narrowed. "I understand. Have you put yourself at risk to tell me this?"

He paused for a moment more. "Then don't call me again. Send an e-mail to Tom and he'll get in touch with us if necessary." He paused once more, and then added, "Thank you, Father. Take care."

"What's going on?" I demanded. "Was that Father Andrew?"

Simon nodded and signaled the waiter for the check. "Yes," he said. "We've got to get out of Scotland right now."

"What's the problem?" I asked.

"I don't know precisely," he said. "All he said is that we are in danger here and we need to get away." The server brought the check and Simon paid in cash. "Send Tom a note telling him to expect contact from Father Andrew, and that he should get in touch with you right away if he does."

I pulled the BlackBerry out of my pack and turned it on. The signal came on and I jotted a quick e-mail:

Dear Tom—

Please check your email regularly for contact from Father Andrew. We aren't sure what's going on, but Simon thought it might be dangerous for him to contact us directly, so we need to rely on you to be the go-between.

If you hear from him, please get in touch right away.

Sorry to add to your burdens, and hope you are safe and well.

Always,

Jenna

"Got it?" Simon asked as I finished.

"Yes," I said. "Now what?"

"Now we go." He stood, and picked up our luggage. "We're already booked on a flight to London, but maybe we can catch an earlier one."

"Did Father Andrew say anything else?" I followed

Simon out of the restaurant and into the lobby of the hotel.

"No," Simon said. "He sounded like he was on a pay phone and in a hurry. I pray he is safe. If he suspects danger, then he took a great risk to call us."

"But who or what could he have met or seen or heard that would be a danger to us?" I asked.

Simon walked out of the lobby doors and tossed our luggage into the back seat of the rental car. "I don't know for sure," he said. "And that worries me."

We drove to the airport quickly, with Simon looking behind us as much as he did in front of us. Before he got us killed, I said, "Do you want me to look behind us so you can focus on the road ahead?"

He grinned, and shook his head. "Not really. I'll probably be nervous until we're actually headed for London. I may not even feel better then."

"At least you're honest."

We made it to the airport without a problem and Simon was able to change our tickets to an earlier flight. After checking our luggage and suffering through the security screening, we found a place to wait that allowed Simon to watch everyone that came near us with a skeptical eye.

Eventually, we boarded our flight and it was only when we were seated and taxiing out to the runway that Simon breathed a sigh of relief and seemed to relax. I'd never seen him so uptight, but I decided not to press him about it.

"Good," Shalizander said. *"I see you are learning discretion."*

"I've been waiting for you," I said. *"Even the Boards have been quiet lately. You'd all better be careful—I don't know what I'd do with all this time to myself."*

"I wanted you to have some time to consider the situation in peace," she said. *"I hope you understand that the ritual is the only way. Even Malizander would have told you this."*

I thought about what she said, and realized that she didn't know what Malizander had told me. *"She mentioned it,"* I admitted, thinking fast, *"but our discussion was focused on other things."*

"Other things?"

"Your prophecy," I said. *"She told me the full version."*

Shalizander laughed. *"No, my daughter,"* she said, *"she told you the version I gave to her. There's far more to it than what she ever knew."*

Here we go again, I thought. *"What do you mean?"*

"I mean that when whatever moved me to speak those words, I was alone. I shared the parts of the prophecy that I thought best, but not all of it. Not even close to all of it. Think on that for a time, and then ask yourself how important knowing it will be when you face Malkander."

And then she would say no more. The Boards and Shalizander were all silent, but in its own way, that was now worse than their usual strident chorus.

Knowing I couldn't trust her, that she *wanted* to possess me and take over the quest for the Boards, made it possible to tell myself she was probably lying about the prophecy. But *not* telling the whole thing would be just like her, too.

She's cornered me, I realized, into a place where eventually I'll have to trust her, or die at Malkander's hands.

London's Heathrow Airport was a vast maze that made most major airports in the United States look easy to navigate. Though it only contained four terminals, it was by far the busiest airport I'd ever been in. A chaotic mass of people crowded the hallways, stopping in duty-free shops and restaurants and talking on their cell phones in a hundred different languages.

I was more than glad to follow Simon through customs, where Armand waited for us.

As always, he was in a tailored suit; this one was dark blue, almost black, with elegant silver pinstripes. He wore a crisp, white shirt and a red silk tie.

"Jenna," he said, wrapping me in a hug. "I'm glad you're safe. I understand you have the stone?"

I nodded, and Simon said, "We can discuss that later, Armand. I won't feel comfortable until we're safely away from here."

"It's unlikely you were followed," he said, "but I understand your concern. Come with me."

We followed him outside, where a luxury car waited.

"I have a home here," he explained as we got in, "so at least you'll be spared another less-than-stellar hotel room for now."

"That sounds wonderful," I said. "But do you have Internet access?"

"All the wonders of the modern world, and a few more beyond that."

On the way, we quickly filled him in on our time in Scotland, as well as Father Andrew's phone call. He seemed as concerned as Simon was about the call, but focused even more on the two men who had broken into my room. "That doesn't fit with how our enemies usually work," he concluded. "I'm not sure what to make of it."

Neither was I, and I said so. Our conversation turned to Armand's research on Merlin as we finished the trip.

I wasn't sure what I expected Armand's house to be like, but it wasn't what I had imagined. It was a gated estate, just south of London, complete with staff and security people patrolling the grounds. A large stone structure, it looked like it had been here a few centuries, and I could easily imagine the knights of old, perhaps a feudal lord, setting up a residence there.

The walls were gray stone bricks, with vines

and creeping roses working their way up the side of the main building. A smooth, circular drive led us to the front doors, while behind us, the security gates swung shut on silent hinges.

"Armand, it's . . . amazing," I said, as we got out of the car. "It's a . . ."

"Castle," Simon supplied as he removed our bags from the trunk over the polite protests of Armand's driver. "He lives in a castle."

"A castle, please," Armand objected. "This is more like a cottage."

"How many bedrooms?" Simon asked quickly.

"Well, there's twelve, plus the master suite," Armand said, his cheeks turning red.

"That is a castle," I said. "But I think it's wonderful."

"So do I," he replied. "It's one of the better perks to my job as the leader of the Templars."

"You get perks?" Simon asked.

"Not many," Armand replied, "but more than you do." He gestured toward the front door, which looked more like something that should have been on the other side of a moat. "Shall we?"

We followed him inside, and that evening, after we had cleaned up and had a chance to rest, we had dinner cooked by a chef and served by Armand's staff. I'd never enjoyed such hospitality in my life, and the food—five courses, including a wilted greens salad and fork-tender beef Wellington, all served with various wines—was heavenly.

Our conversation during the meal was light as

Simon matched wits with his old friend. Their discussion, which seemed to be a long-running argument between them, centered on whether or not William Shakespeare had actually written all those plays and poems or if he was a phony. Armand took the side of Shakespeare, while Simon gleefully poked holes in his arguments.

In between passes with Simon, Armand played host, telling us about his home and how, as it turned out, I had been right. It had once belonged to a landed knight, a minor noble, and his family.

Over dessert—a sweet confection of angel food cake drizzled with some kind of chocolate-raspberry puree—our conversation turned more serious. First, we filled him in on the prophecy and the fact that Shalizander was still alive, in a bizarre way, but very much a force to be reckoned with.

He copied down the words of the prophecy and pursed his lips. "There's something familiar here," he said. "The line 'That protects the hidden Boundary, buried deep beneath the Land.' I've heard that before, but can't think of where."

"Don't force it," Simon suggested. "It will come to you. Probably in the middle of the night."

"Probably," Armand said. "I'll think on it some and if it comes to me, I'll let you know. For now, let us turn our attention to Merlin's tomb. It could be in several locations. We're going to have to search for it."

"We should start tomorrow then." Simon sipped

his after-dinner coffee and looked relaxed for the first time in days. He wore faded jeans and an old cream-colored sweater that looked very used, and very comfortable. "Jenna, have you heard it calling for you, yet?"

I shook my head. "No, but I haven't really tried. The Boards have been exceptionally quiet, so I'll give it a shot before bed. Why they've been quiet is beyond me. They usually talk my ear off."

"Perhaps you should try now," he suggested. "If you could pinpoint the location, we won't have to waste time searching."

I yawned and stretched. For some reason I'd never been able to identify, using the Boards when I had to or when the situation seemed urgent felt fine. Using them on demand was embarrassing. Maybe because I'd learned from my grandfather that a person who *uses* power is often weaker than a person who withholds her strength.

Armand must have sensed my reluctance because he rose to his feet—and my rescue. "Simon, Jenna's obviously tired. She can do it in the morning, in private, and let us know if she discovers anything." He turned to me. "Thank you for gracing my home, my dear. I've had a lovely evening."

I stood and smiled. For all that everyone seemed to think Armand was a bit pompous and arrogant—or as my great-grandfather Dario had called him, a stuffed shirt—he had always been kind to me, and a gentleman.

"As did I," I said. "Thank you for a wonderful

meal. I haven't felt this full or this safe in weeks."

"Within these walls, you are safe, Jenna," he said. "That much, I can promise you."

"Good night, Jenna," Simon said.

I called good night to him and went to my room. I was tired, but the truth was more complicated than that. I didn't want to open myself up to Shalizander and the Boards again. Not when they were finally quiet. Even putting it off for a few hours seemed like a blessed decision.

I shut the door to my room, changed out of my clothes and climbed beneath the covers.

Unused to Shalizander and the Boards being so quiet, I fell into sleep and once more crossed the boundaries between the worlds, hoping to meet with the wizard called Emrys.

This time, however, he was already waiting for me.

"I don't understand—they've holed up in Armand's house, and don't seem to be doing anything."

"Patience! They plot their next moves even as we speak."

"But shouldn't we take them now? They would never expect it at this moment. My team could be ready to go within the hour—"

"Have you learned nothing? They have come this far, and they will lead you to the Board. In the meantime, I'm sending someone to assist your men. He's quite talented and will make sure they do as you've instructed them."

"I thought we had agreed that I would handle this part of things."

"The situation has changed. You will recall that you've already lost your 'best' men. I'm sending one of mine."

The circled stones are flawless rectangles, massive in scope and towering over my head. Each is cov-

ered with hundreds, perhaps thousands, of runes and symbols. Some are so close together that in the blood-red sunset, I cannot make them out.

Directly in front of me is a large stone slab, squared off and made of what appears to be some kind of lava rock. Merlin Emrys sits on this altar, a smile on his face. His robes are brown and gray, and he carelessly holds a long, rune-marked staff in one hand. His hair and beard are pure white, and his eyes a piercing blue-gray that reminds me of a storm at sea.

All around us, the land is quiet and still. Beyond the outer circle of stones, I see that all the trees have been cleared away.

"You near the end of your quest, Keeper," he says. "I sense that you have recovered the phoenix stone, and will soon begin your search for my final resting place." He stands up and grips his staff. "I am pleased."

"Good," I say. "It wasn't easy, by the way. Coghlan was there."

"After all these long years?" Merlin says, his voice filled with surprise. "I did not imagine he had such powers."

"I don't think he did either," I reply. "I think his hate and anger and desire for the Boards sustained his soul in this world, long after his body and mind had rotted away."

"Often we underestimate the power of emotions," he says. "True love or heartfelt hate can contain a force that surpasses even magic." He peered around

the circle of stones. "What do you think of it?" he asks.

"It looks a lot like Stonehenge," I say. "Only more . . . finished."

"That's exactly right, Keeper. This—" he gestures around us "—is what Stonehenge was supposed to look like when it was complete. Alas, I never got the chance. My loyalty to my own vision, and the man you think of as Arthur, got me killed before that could happen."

"Merlin," I say, "Stonehenge has existed in one form or another since . . ."

"About 3000 B.C., as you calculate time," he supplies. "Time has a different meaning for people like me. I got around more than most. Call me Emrys. Merlin was a fiction invented to make Arthur and his people more comfortable."

"And your father," I say, recalling Malizander's words.

"So you have uncovered the truth," he says. "Yes, the man you call Malkander was my father. My mother was a daemon, a succubus. I was a failed experiment. He sought to circumvent the prophecy by fathering a son who was not constrained by the usual boundaries of mortals."

"Like an incubus? But I thought they didn't have the, ummm . . . right equipment to . . . you know."

"On the human plane of existence, they don't," he says. "Malkander traveled to her home."

I shudder, trying to imagine what such a place

might be like. And what kind of power it would take to do that.

"Time grows ever shorter, Keeper," Merlin—or rather Emrys—says. "My tomb is what you see here. Located at the place you call Stonehenge. You are to go there and bring the phoenix stone and all of the Boards with you. It is time for you to receive the next portion of your inheritance."

"Stonehenge doesn't look anything like this place now," I say. "It's a regular place visited by tourists. How will I find your tomb there?"

"You have all the resources you need to find me," he says. "And come at a time when the uninitiated have better things to do. Like sleep." He turns and walks away.

"Wait!" I say. "I have more questions."

"The young always do," he says over his shoulder. "You think when you should act, and act when you should think. Go now, Keeper, and remember that when you claim the final Board, you will be but a step away from complete mastery of the elements—an achievement that eluded even me."

A shadow moves across the stones and he is gone.

Behind me, the sun flares crimson through the stones and I am momentarily blinded. The only color I can see is red. Like an arterial flow of blood that covers the world. I wonder if this vision is what Emrys intended when he designed this place.

I rub my eyes, open them and I . . .

. . . woke up to the midnight silence of Armand's home on the outskirts of London.

My room was dark, and through the window, I saw the moon illuminating the grounds outside. Large trees and hedges made a maze of the one side of the house, and once there was the sharp bark of a dog patrolling the grounds. I tensed, remembering the would-be assassins in Scotland, but no other sounds came and the dog remained silent.

Tentatively, I reached out with my mind for the Board of the Waters. Of the three Boards in my possession, it had been the most helpful and the least trouble.

"I am the Keeper of the Boards. My will is your will."

It responded immediately. *"What is your will, Keeper?"*

"Information," I said. *"Why have you and your brothers remained so quiet, when before all you did was talk to me and each other?"*

"Such reticence was the desire of the Creator, Shalizander."

"Why?"

"To permit you time to consider her desire that you complete the ritual of the dagger."

"Then you're going to be quiet a long time because I won't do it," I said.

"Not yet, perhaps, but in time you will see that it is necessary, should you wish to fulfill your destiny and should you wish to live."

"Do you threaten me?" I asked.

"No," the Board replied. *"But the challenges you will face in securing the remaining Boards as well as the dangers that will be thrown in your path by Malkander* will *do so. Without Shalizander's powers, you will eventually falter. And then, you will die."*

"I have allies," I said. *"People that are helping me."*

"Even the greatest warrior can be overcome should sufficient forces engage him all at once."

I thought about this and realized it was true. Sooner or later, Malkander would throw everything he had at us. And then people—people I loved and cared about—would die. Since the Board seemed willing to talk, I changed direction. *"There is something else I would know."*

"I will tell you anything allowed to me," the Board said, *"provided you ask the right questions."*

"Who or what could constrain you?"

"Many things, Keeper. The prophecy, Shalizander or Malkander, the Master, limited information."

"The Master? Who is that?"

"The Master is he who brought about the destruction wrought by our creation. It was his hand that caused the magic to go awry."

"There is someone more powerful in this than Shalizander or Malkander?" I asked.

"They are but motes in the Master's eye," it said. *"A tiny flicker of power, compared to his own."*

"Do they know who he is?"

"Yes," it said. *"Even now, Malkander schemes with him."*

"I don't understand," I said. *"Are you saying that Malkander serves him?"*

The Board laughed, and the sound was the same as a trickling brook. *"Malkander is enslaved by him."*

"And the Boards?" I asked. *"Are you also enslaved by the Master?"*

There was a long silence, then, *"We are a part of the Master."*

"What does that mean?"

"At the moment of our creation, the Master placed a spark of himself—a piece, one might say—of his essence, within the magical framework of each Board. Those wizards involved in our creation believed they were capturing elementals and prime forces. Malkander betrayed them all by arranging for the Master to intervene."

"So, then, what are *you?"* I asked, afraid to hear the answer. *"Who is the Master?"*

The Board laughed once more. *"You have already asked this question, Keeper, and been answered."*

"I think," Shalizander's voice said, *"that you've learned more than enough for one evening."*

I heard a muttered word that was barely pronounceable, let alone understandable, and the Board of the Waters went silent.

"Daughter, perhaps these questions are best asked of one who was there?"

"You don't give me answers," I said. *"Only more questions. You only share what you have to."*

"I share what you are ready to hear and understand," she said. *"One does not burden the apprentice with the secrets of the universe before the apprentice has mastered the secrets of her own abilities."*

"I'm not asking for the secrets of the universe!" I shouted. *"I just want to understand all this."*

"In time, you will," she said. *"But for now, I believe I will leave you to the less tender mercies of the Boards."* She muttered a few brief words, and then I heard her say, *"Grametex!"*

For a moment, silence descended, then all the Boards began talking to me at once.

It was so noisy and chaotic that my head pounded, and I couldn't even make out whatever they were saying. I rolled over and screamed into my pillow, praying that no one in the house would hear me.

I didn't bother trying to sleep for the rest of the night. I knew the Boards wouldn't let me.

Shortly after sunrise, I left my room with a throbbing headache and the voices of the Boards echoing in my head. For now, they'd stopped talking to me and were reserving most of their comments for each other, using a mix of English and the Language of the Birds. They'd figured out that if they interspersed a recognizable word once in a while, it was harder for me to tune them out.

Simon and Armand sat in the dining room, drinking coffee and talking quietly. On the table, breakfast was waiting in the form of a large platter of sweet pastries and a bowl of fruit, with a tin of cream on the side. My stomach roiled at the very thought of eating.

"Good morning, Jenna," Armand said as he rose. "I hope you slept well."

"As do I," Simon said. "I feel terrible that you've been unable to really rest since this started."

I stared at both men, doing my best to stop my head from spinning, then found my way to a chair and sat.

"Sleep," I said, "is for the weak. Who needs sleep when I have such a good time staying awake all night and listening to the Boards jabber at me and each other in the Language of the Birds?"

Simon poured me a cup of coffee and Armand looked at me, worry etched across his face. I waved a hand at them and said, "Never mind, I'm just tired. I would have slept, if the Boards and Shalizander had let me. The room was wonderful."

"I'm sorry that you are struggling so much with the Boards," Armand said. "If there was more I could do, I would."

"Hopefully, once we find Merlin's tomb and retrieve the final Board, you will get some much needed peace," Simon added.

"How about a vacation?" I asked hopefully.

"Some place warm with shopping, a day spa, and a 'No Evil Wizards for 100 miles' policy?"

The two men laughed, and I felt some of the tension drain from my shoulders.

"I can't promise the last one," Simon said, "but as we don't know where to even begin searching for the next set of Boards, I had been thinking that a break might be a good thing for both of us. Armand and I discussed it last night, and he's arranged for us to spend some time at one of his retreats in the south of France when we're done here."

"It's a lovely place, Jenna," Armand said. "And I'll see to it that you're pampered to your heart's content."

"Thank you," I said to them both. "It . . . it means a lot to me that you even thought of it."

"We're not heartless, Jenna," Simon said. "Just a little more driven than most people. A requirement of our unique circumstances."

"Indeed," Armand said. "Which brings us back to the here and now. There are several locations we can search for Merlin's final resting place."

"His real name *was* Emrys," I interrupted. "And his tomb is in Stonehenge."

Both men stopped and stared at me. I shrugged. "I never said there weren't some benefits to all the racket in my head and the disrupted sleep."

"It makes sense," Armand admitted. "Merlin—excuse me, Emrys—has long been associated with it. There has even been speculation that he built it."

"He did," I said, "but was never able to complete it. It's probably a good thing, too, because if he had, I'm pretty certain it would be a much different place today."

"Still," Simon said, "Stonehenge has been explored by hundreds of archaeologists and thousands of tourists. If the tomb is there, finding it won't be that easy."

Armand nodded, and I was once again struck by how he always looked perfectly dressed. Not a single strand of his raven black hair was out of place, and he wore a perfectly knotted silk tie even at breakfast in his own home.

"Agreed," he said. "It won't be in an obvious place and is probably hidden by magical means."

"I thought so, too," I said. "But Emrys said I had all the resources I needed to figure it out. When the Boards and Shalizander weren't distracting me last night, I gave it some thought. There must be an answer in the Chronicle itself."

Simon refilled everyone's coffee cups. "But he wasn't a Keeper. We don't even know how he got the Board of the Earth. Why would there be anything in the Chronicle related to him?"

"I don't know," I admitted. "But it's the only source I can think of that might address it, short of spending hours and hours in old libraries digging through ancient books and scrolls and hoping to find something that gives us a clue."

Simon frowned. "You're just trying to avoid spending time in any library."

"You're right," I admitted. "And if there's nothing in the Chronicle, you'll get your heart's desire to spend countless days among musty books. I think I should try this first, though."

"She's right, Simon," Armand said. "We could spend years in research or crawling all over Stonehenge and not find anything."

"All right," Simon agreed. "But I still hate the effect it has on you."

"That makes two of us," I said. "But it's in the job description somewhere."

"The fine print," Armand suggested. "The *very* fine print."

I pulled my backpack off the floor and removed the Chronicle. "Normally, I'd do this in my room, but I'm getting better at skimming the text and finding what I need without collapsing. Besides, I'm too tired to hike all the way back."

"Is there anything you need?" Armand asked.

"No," I said. "Except maybe a English–to–Language of the Birds dictionary for when I'm trying to figure out what the Boards are saying."

"She gets sarcastic when she's tired," Simon said. "After a while, it becomes charming."

"Does it?" Armand asked innocently.

I saw that the two of them were teasing me to make me feel better, and I smiled. "Okay, if you two are finished, here we go."

I opened the Chronicle, and began skimming pages, barely reading a word before moving on to the next one. Little snippets of visions tried to gain a foothold in my mind, but I kept my eyes moving before they could materialize.

Finally, a phrase leaped out at me. It read, *"The circle of stones glowed red . . ."*

And I allowed the vision to take me.

The rocks are weathered, the carvings incomplete or nonexistent. Several of the stones have fallen or been tipped over, and the ground is covered with the tracks of countless feet.

Emrys stands near the altar, his robes dirty and frayed. As always, his eyes are tired and sad. "This is the only way."

"I know," I say. "The time for the Daughter of Destiny has not yet come. She will be born many generations from now, long after I, too, am dust."

"I can feel how much you want the power, Morgan," Emrys says, "but it is not for you, anymore than it is for me."

"I understand," I say. "I will do what you have asked of me, though I do not like the role the bards will cast me in."

"Who cares what the bards say a hundred years from now?" Emrys asks. "This is the only way to protect the Board of the Earth from my father—and yes, even from you."

"As we have already agreed, Emrys," I say. "Get on with it."

"Very well," he says. "Between us there is no love lost, I know. But still . . . I thank you. In the course

of time, what we do now will bring the Board of the Earth back to the Daughter of Destiny."

"You are welcome, my old enemy," I say softly. I am surprised to feel a kind of love welling inside me for this man I have hated so long, and a sadness that I am losing him.

"My magic fades quickly," he says. "Bring the Board of the Winds to the altar."

I step forward, carrying the Board in my hands. "Place it on the very center—see the markings?—and watch!"

Directly behind the altar, a shimmering light takes shape. Emerald greens swirl with dandelion yellows, and together they form a rectangle of color hanging still in the air. "A portal!" I say.

"Indeed," says Emrys.

"Is this the opening of the way that the Boards speak of?" I ask. "Do you intend to cross into some other plane of existence?"

"No," the Board of the Winds says in my mind. "That particular altar is far from here, Keeper, and the opening of the way requires that you possess all thirteen Boards and the key."

I don't bother replying to the Board, because asking it for clarification will be a waste of time.

Emrys walks around the altar to stand in front of the blue-tinged portal.

"Farewell, Morgan," he says. "And remember to record all this in the Chronicle."

"I won't fail, Emrys," I say, saddened to see him

leaving, though I can sense how much pain he is in. He is slowly dying, his magics unraveling around him even now. "Rest well, my old enemy. My friend."

"I intend to," Emrys says, and then he steps through the portal and disappears.

I pick up the Board of the Winds from the altar and the portal disappears. I will write all this down in the Chronicle as I promised him, but that doesn't mean I don't ache for the power I have lost today. All the Boards should be mine, I think, but destiny has chosen another. . . .

I opened my eyes and looked at Armand and Simon, as my stomach did flips and rolls. There was a glass of water on the table and I picked it up and sipped carefully. My headache from earlier had eased somewhat, but I was still very tired.

The revelation that Morgan Le Fay had been one of my ancestors was only slightly less disturbing than not knowing where the portal would lead when I opened it.

Simon cleared his throat and both men looked at me expectantly.

"I know how to do it," I said. "But it won't be easy."

"Tell us," Armand said.

So I did, and after their shock that Morgan Le Fay was not only real but also an ancestor of mine, we all agreed that it would be best to go to Stonehenge late at night, in the hopes that we could avoid being seen.

I had a cup of coffee and even choked down what would have normally been a delicious muffin before returning to my room in the hopes of getting some desperately needed rest. It didn't matter what we had decided downstairs, I thought, as I shut the door.

This was one journey I'd be taking alone.

"Your man arrived and took charge of my agents at the scene."

"Excellent. Now all we must do is wait."

"My men report that there's something strange about the person you sent."

"He's obedient, and that is all you or your men need to know."

"He isn't human, is he?"

"Not as you understand the term, no."

The room Armand had provided for me was on the ground floor, with two large windows overlooking the gardens on one side of the main house. It was still early in the day, and I looked outside to see perfectly trimmed rose hedges just beginning to bloom. A splash of red here, yellow there, even the occasional white showed that spring had finally arrived.

I opened the windows and breathed in the cool, scented air. The sun was beginning to warm the day, and I relished the glow on my face. On the far side of the grounds, near the fence line, I saw two men walking together. Both wore a dark uniform and carried heavy, wooden batons. Periodically, they would stop and examine the fence or make a minor adjustment to an unseen device hidden within the foliage. Apparently Armand took his security very seriously.

Leaving the windows open, I curled up in an overstuffed chair and thought about what I'd learned since that afternoon in my grandfather's attic when I'd found and awakened the Board of the Winds for the first time. Now that I possessed three Boards and was about to go after the fourth and final Board of the first set, now seemed like a good time to try and organize all of the pieces of the millennia-old puzzle I had inherited.

I knew that the Boards had been created by a group of sorcerers working together in the massive Tower of Babel, and that something had gone awry, killing all those involved except my ultimate ancestor, Shalizander, and her secret lover, Malkander. I knew that Malkander had betrayed those involved and disappeared soon after, leaving Shalizander to try and control the Boards, then destroy them. Sometime thereafter, both of them had uttered prophecies that somehow seemed to bind them both to a specific set of circumstances regarding the Boards. Each, apparently, had seen a different version of the future. It was unclear, however, where the prophecies originated from—Shalizander and Malkander themselves, or some other entity.

I also knew that Shalizander had decided to hide

all the Boards—except the Board of the Winds, which she had kept for herself and her heirs—in various places throughout the world. Some, it seemed, had been found and lost again. Some, perhaps, had never been found. In order to accomplish this, Shalizander had extended her own life through the use of an enchanted dagger that allowed her to transfer her spirit into her daughter's body. With Malizander's aid, the Boards had been hidden, and Shalizander had preserved herself through the centuries in another plane of existence.

Her bloodline had proven strong, and each generation had produced one female offspring, down through the many centuries, finally leading to me. I was the last of her line, and the supposed Daughter of Destiny—a name that still made my teeth ache when I thought about it too much.

As for her lover and enemy, Malkander had a strong bloodline too, producing a new male son once every hundred years until he produced twins—my enemy Peraud, whose spirit was now being held by Shalizander, and Simon Monk, who I could love with all my heart, but who had chosen to remain faithful to his vows as a priest.

Finally, I knew that the Boards desired something called the opening of the way, and that they apparently were a part of someone or something they believed was their Master—even more powerful than Malkander and Shalizander. They would stop at nothing to make me do what they wanted, and neither would their Mistress, Shalizander.

Collectively, they believed that in order for me to fulfill my destiny and face the challenges ahead, I would have to perform the same ritual that Malizander had done, allowing Shalizander to enter my body and my mind—to possess me—so that she could use her magical abilities to ensure the success of my quest.

Already, she had tried to use me that way once and nearly killed Simon in the process. Throughout this journey, it seemed I had always been more passive than active. Going where I was told and doing what Simon and Armand wanted me to do. My best friend Tom had been paralyzed when I lost control of the first Board. So many others had sacrificed for me and risked their lives, and I had blithely gone along with it all.

The question I asked myself at that moment was why? And the answer, I realized—and was sorry to admit—was fear. I was afraid to be alone—really, truly alone—and afraid to take responsibility for what I had to do as the Keeper of the Boards. Some day, maybe, I'd learn more about my mother and my grandmother, neither of whom had been given the chance to tell me what I needed to know.

But that was someday. Right now I needed to embrace my name—Solitaire—and take responsibility for myself. It wasn't right to risk others simply because I was afraid. In my heart, I had to keep myself walled off more than I had, or other people would get hurt, and maybe even killed.

The only thing I could do was to go to Merlin's tomb, alone. There didn't seem to be any reason to bring Simon or Armand and risk them unnecessarily. To keep them safe was the very least I could do, after all they had done for me. Besides, if there were any dangers, I was more than capable of using the Boards to defend myself. It was time, I realized, to act like my grandfather would have expected me to act. I needed to lead and be my own person, not just follow the lead of others.

I focused my will and called out, *"Shalizander!"*

She replied almost immediately. *"Yes, my daughter?"*

"Stop calling me that," I said. *"You aren't even close to being my mother. Jenna will do fine."*

"As you wish . . . Jenna," she said. *"I sense that you have more to say."*

"I do," I said. *"You need to stop badgering me and stop telling the Boards what to do and not do. I'm never going to be able to figure this out for myself if you keep interfering."*

"If you'd only complete—"

"No! I'm not doing the damn ritual. If it comes to that, I'll figure it out then. Right now, I just want to get the fourth Board. I need to do it on my own, and I'll need the Boards to cooperate. They won't do that if they're taking orders from you."

"I seek only to help you, Jenna," she said, her voice soothing. *"I understand the challenges you face."*

"That's where you're wrong," I said. *"You*

understand the challenges you *faced. But you're dead, and have been for a long time. I'm alive, and whether you like it or not, I am the Daughter of Destiny and the Keeper of the Boards, not you."*

I got the impression that she was taken back a bit by this statement.

"You have not misnamed yourself, Jenna, but I created the Boards, and only I know all their secrets."

"Goody for you," I snapped. *"But you seem to keep forgetting that I don't care about that. Let me put it this way. If you continue to interfere, then I will stop my quest. I'll drop the Boards into the ocean or into a volcano or whatever and even if it drives me insane, even if it kills me, I will go no farther. That will be it."*

A long silence greeted this pronouncement, and then, *"Very well, Jenna. I will cease my attempts to influence you, and I will tell the Boards that they are to respond to you as their nature and construction dictate."*

"Good," I said. *"That's all for now."*

"You are . . . dismissing me?" she asked.

There was a hint of menace in her words, but I had come too far to back out now.

"Yes, I am," I said. *"I don't have anything else to say to you at the moment."*

"As you wish . . . Keeper of the Boards."

As quickly as she'd responded, she was gone from my mind. And just as quick, the Boards spoke to me.

"Well done, Keeper," the Board of the Waters said. *"You are learning what it is to be the fulfillment of a prophecy."*

"To choose your own path is wisdom," the Board of the Winds said. *"To follow a path chosen for you is folly."*

"Each day, your strength grows, Keeper," the Board of the Flames rumbled. *"I am . . . impressed."*

"Thank you," I replied. *"Now all of you take a hint from your Mistress and shut up so I can think."*

The Boards went silent, and I contemplated how I was going to get away from here without being caught by one of the security guards or letting Simon or Armand know what I was doing.

I would have to do some creative lying to put them at ease. Somehow, this thought made me more uncomfortable than anything else I had considered so far.

It was one thing, I knew, to lie to enemies and those you couldn't trust. It was quite another to lie to your friends.

After a quiet day of research and rest, Armand, Simon, and I all agreed to leave for Stonehenge late that night. I made excuses to go and rest, and the house was quiet as they did the same. Knowing that I was taking some risks, I turned on my BlackBerry and got online to send a quick message to Tom and Kristen, using BCC to hide the e-mail addresses.

> Dear T & K—
>
> I so wish I were there to help you both. I know that you are struggling right now, but I also know that if you focus on the feelings that you both have for each other, there is no challenge you cannot overcome together.
>
> I love you both.
>
> Take care,
>
> Jenna

I read the message over, and then hit the SEND button. It was the best I could do for them until I had recovered the Board of the Earth and maybe had a chance to go home. I could only hope that whatever was really going on with them would turn out okay.

I put the BlackBerry away and slipped on my leather jacket and backpack. I'd already decided to leave my meager amount of luggage at the house. If I was successful, I'd come back for it, and if I failed, I wouldn't need it. There was no reason to burden myself with anything extra right now.

I stepped over to the windows, which I had left open earlier, and looked into the gardens. Night had fallen, and pretty soon Armand or Simon would be knocking on my door. I needed to leave, and the best way seemed to be right here. I slid the chair over, stepped on the seat, and carefully climbed out, trying to be as quiet as possible. I didn't want to attract the attention of Armand's dogs or his security people, though I suspected that they would be looking for someone trying to break in, not out.

Outside, I stepped into the gardens themselves, and called on the Board of the Winds. *"I am the Keeper of the Boards. My will is your will."*

The Board responded quickly. *"What is your will, Keeper?"*

"I require a wind to lift me up, over the gardens and the fence, and into the street beyond."

"Your will is my will, Keeper," it replied.

Almost immediately, the trees stirred as a strong wind swirled across the estate. I watched from the shadows as two of the security staff ran by to secure a loose tarp flapping on a woodpile near the far end of the gardens.

The wind grew stronger, and I felt it spin more tightly around me.

"Lift me up," I commanded.

Slowly, I rose into the air, and prayed that no one would bother looking up, but would be focused on securing the grounds. *"Higher, faster!"* I ordered.

The magic of the Board flared once more and the wind's strength increased. The dogs barked wildly, no doubt sensing the strange phenomenon, but neither they nor anyone else apparently saw me. The winds swirled faster still, and I floated into the night sky, a shadow among the trees as I passed over the gardens and the fence surrounding Armand's property.

"Excellent," I said to the Board. *"Now lower me to the ground."*

"As you will, Keeper," it replied. *"We are all pleased with your progress."*

I ignored this last comment—a couple of compliments now weren't going to get them on my good side anytime soon. The winds faded, and I slowly drifted to the ground, standing in the middle of a quiet road. On the other side of the fence, I heard one of the two guards say, "What do you make of that?"

The second one replied, "I bloody well don't. We work for Armand and we don't ask questions about the weather or much of anything else."

I smiled and started jogging at a good clip. If I was lucky, I'd be able to hitch a ride back to Heathrow—and the nearest car rental counter.

For once, good fortune was on my side, as I was quickly able to hitch a ride with a kindly old British gentleman who looked like he was torn between picking me up and running for his life. He was very polite and asked hardly any questions, and dropped me outside the doors of Heathrow. I went inside and rented a small car, thankful that I still had a credit card linked to my trust account back in the States. I filled out the forms and negligently told the woman that I had driven in England before, and then headed outside to pick up the car and leave the airport.

After a couple of near-accidents, complete with blaring horns and shouted curses, I got it into my head that I needed to drive on the opposite side of the road. I quickly learned that driving that way, especially at night, requires a lot of concentration, and I got turned around a few times before I found the road to Amesbury, the small town near Stonehenge.

A short time later, I pulled the car to a stop when I could see the stone monument in the distance. The full moon illuminated the site nicely, and there didn't appear to be anyone else around. Still, I thought it would be smart to leave the car here, so that it didn't look like someone was parked right next to the ancient monument.

I got out and grabbed my backpack, then set out at a jog once more. It wasn't very far, and I could easily see where I was going. Once I reached the site and climbed over the single strand of chain ringing the perimeter, I moved through the two outer rings of rocks quickly, but discovered that a high chain-link fence had been built around the inner ring. I walked the entire length of the fence looking for an opening, but all I found was a padlocked gate.

Just as I was about to call on the Boards, I heard a soft footstep behind me. I spun, ready to call on the Boards to incinerate whoever was about to attack me, only to see Simon and Armand approaching. I released my held breath in a *whoosh,* too relieved to be angry with the two men for sneaking up on me and almost getting themselves killed.

"Don't you think," Simon said, "that you should have waited for us?"

"I didn't want you to come," I said, annoyed at the sense of relief I felt now that he was here. "I didn't want to put anyone else at risk."

"That, my dear," Armand said, "is our choice, is it not?"

"But both of you will always choose the risk, and I . . . I don't want anyone else getting hurt on my behalf. It's time I took my responsibilities more seriously."

Simon stepped close and put a hand on my shoulder. "Jenna, Armand and I know the risks we're taking. In some ways, even better than you, because we've been at this for quite a while."

"And we choose to take them anyway," Armand added. "You have a responsibility to the Boards, but also to your friends."

"Risk is a part of true friendship," Simon said, "even if it means our lives are in danger. The goals we pursue together are worth the risks we take."

I looked at these two men who were so much a part of my life now, both of them so willing to be my friend, even when it could be me who hurt them—and found myself smiling. I stepped into

Simon's arms and hugged him tightly. He was calm and confident and warm, and once again, I realized how much I loved him—and that having him as my friend was just as important as anything else we might have been.

I moved out of his embrace and hugged Armand, too. He laughed quietly, and squeezed me once, then gently pushed me back.

"We're all in this together, right?" he asked.

"Yes," I said. "Together."

"Good," he said. He picked up a leather bag at his feet, unzipped it, and dug around inside. "We'll be needing these, then," he added, holding up a pair of bolt cutters.

Simon took them and quickly cut the padlocks securing the gate. The hinges made a horrific squealing sound when he opened it, and I almost jumped out of my skin. Armand chuckled, and said, "Let's go."

We slipped through the gate, and passed through the inner ring of stones to where the central altar stone was located.

"Okay," Simon said. "You obviously had a plan when you got here, so what is it?"

I set down my backpack and removed the three Boards and the phoenix stone.

"My plan isn't anything special," I said. "In my vision, all I had to do was set the boards in the center of the altar."

"It's a start," Simon said, removing a high-intensity flashlight from his waist pack. "Maybe there are markings on the altar that will show you more."

I walked up to the altar stone and saw that it was covered in patchy lichen. "Hold on a second." I scrubbed with one hand at the greenish growth. "These stones are old."

The lichen flaked away, and I saw that underneath it were very faint, almost invisible markings like those on the Boards.

"Here," I said. "Can you shine the light closer?"

Simon pointed the beam where my fingers were. "Look at that."

Armand tried to peer over our shoulders. "Mind if I take a look?"

"Go ahead." Simon moved back, giving him room.

Peering closely at the marks, Armand said, "Simon, shut off your light. Jenna, move the Boards closer to the stone."

We did as he asked, and the markings became more visible, almost glowing in faint yellow lines. "That explains that, anyway," Armand said.

"Explains what?" I asked, confused.

"Why no one has ever found these runes," he said. "If you move the Boards farther away, they'll fade back into the stone. It's only when the Boards are close that they become visible in the first place."

"Fascinating," Simon said. "Jenna, move the Boards directly over the altar and see what happens."

I did as he suggested, and the runes became even

more visible, bright yellow lines that glowed almost like neon. Then, as we watched, they merged together and moved, slowly settling back onto the surface of the stone, looking for all the world like the outline of the Boards I was holding in my hand.

"Set the Boards down just like the runes show," Armand said.

I set them down and a faint hum filled the air. "Something's happening."

"Yes," Simon said, pointing. "Look!"

Just as it had happened in my vision, colored lights of green and yellow began to swirl in the air, forming a blue-tinted rectangle just behind the altar stone.

"The portal," I said. Even to my ears, my voice sounded dreamy and distant.

As the rectangle solidified, I felt myself pulled in that direction. Not violently, but a gentle tug, and I began to move without thinking about it. I knew that I'd have to step through the portal to find Emrys' tomb.

Simon stepped beside me. "I'm going with you."

I didn't reply, couldn't, as the magic of the portal called to me, compelled me to keep moving.

From a long ways away, I heard Armand say, "Jenna, are you all right?"

I knew I should answer, tell him I was fine, but I reached the portal and stepped through it instead.

There was a brief flare, a rainbow of hues and colors washing across my vision, and then I was on the other side. Alone.

Simon hadn't come through with me, and I wondered if he was all right. I started to turn around, to go back, but the portal itself was gone.

Then, a familiar voice from my dreams spoke. "Worry not, Keeper of the Boards. The portal was created to be a door for only one person—you. Your friends will be fine."

I turned back around and found myself peering into the bright blue eyes of Emrys. They glowed with a faint luminescence in the dark.

I had finally reached the tomb of the one soul who could give me the Board of the Earth, and the key to creating the Master Board of the Elements.

"Stonehenge! Of course! It all makes sense now."

"You can see now why in this case patience was the prudent course of action."

"Apparently they are separated, with the Keeper in some kind of underground chamber or something. I'm sending the team in to subdue Simon and Armand, then we'll bring the Keeper to hand."

"Hmm, that sounds familiar."

"What's that you said?"

"Nothing . . . nothing at all. Good luck . . ."

Emrys's tomb was so dark that it was hard to make out any details. The walls were rough, with jagged edges of stone, and in the center, I barely made out a plain stone bier, topped by a robe-dressed corpse that had turned into bones and dust long ago. The staff I had seen in my dreams lay across the remains, but the dimly lit cavern revealed little else.

"Come, Keeper," Emrys said. "There is much to do, and little time to do it."

"How about a little light?" I asked, stumbling after him.

He muttered a brief word, and a glowing orb appeared in the air in front of us. Suddenly, the entire tomb was brightly lit. The rough-hewn edges of stone were actually hundreds of pieces of raw crystal, and they reflected the light from the orb a thousand times over. I gasped in pleased surprise. "It's . . . breathtaking," I said.

"So I thought, too," he said, "at first. But after this many years, I am more than ready to leave this place for whatever comes next."

I stared at his form, and realized that unlike the man I had seen in my dreams, this was a spirit, albeit a very strong one. In places, he was translucent, just like Coghlan had been.

"Where is the Board of the Earth?" I asked.

He led me over to the bier and pointed at a small outcropping of stone. "Move that away. Interacting with physical objects is more difficult when you are only a spirit."

I knelt down and pulled on the stone, which crumbled in my hands. I used my fingers to claw it out, revealing an opening behind it. I was strangely reminded of where my grandmother had hidden the Chronicle in the pedestal of a Virgin Mary statue at our church. I reached inside and felt the familiar wood of a Board, took a deep breath, then pulled it free.

I felt a surge of triumph. More than any other Board, this one meant the most to me. It meant a chance at something like peace and represented, if nothing else, the end of the beginning.

This was the final piece that would complete the first set of Boards. It was shaped like the others—roughly triangular, with one side of the arc cut out, which dipped down—and as I had seen in my visions, this one had runes that were more nature oriented. One of them was clearly a mountain-like shape, another one looked a bit like grass or maybe wheat, and several looked like rocks or crystals. There were more, and I knew I'd have to study them later. Then something occurred to me.

"Why haven't I heard this Board? It doesn't call out like the others did—or maybe I just couldn't hear it because of the other Boards."

"A good question," Emrys said. "This Board has slept for many long years, and no human has even come close to disturbing its slumber. It tends to react more slowly, I think, than the other Boards in your possession, and awakening it will be more challenging."

"I wonder why?" I muttered, more to myself than to him, but he answered anyway.

"The Earth is patient, Keeper of the Boards," Emrys said. "Perhaps it takes its time because it knows, far better than we ever could, how much time it truly has."

"Maybe," I said, when another thought crossed

my mind. "Why is it that you've stayed here? I mean your spirit."

Emrys smiled grimly. "I didn't really mean to," he said. "Morgan Le Fay—your ancestor, as you have undoubtedly discovered—was supposed to return and reactivate the portal with her Board, allowing me to leave once I had created the necessary protection magics here. Only a Keeper or a Holder can open the portal, and only from the outside. I wanted to leave the Board of the Earth here for safekeeping. She never returned and eventually, I chose to end my existence, rather than continue on in a . . . less-than-pleasant situation."

Hoping he didn't hold a grudge against my family, I grimaced. "So you've been here ever since?"

"This form is transient," he said. "Before my death, I cast spells that would call forth my spirit when the events of the prophecy began to unfold. Thus, I could ensure that the Board of the Earth went to its rightful heir."

"Thank you," I said, and meant it. "At least this one isn't trapped."

"Not exactly, no," he said. "But you still have tasks before you," he replied. "The first is to awaken this Board."

"And the second?"

"All in due time," he said. "Look there." One long, gnarled finger pointed at his corpse on the bier.

"What?" I asked.

"In the left hand outer pocket of my robe is a piece of stone—it's called a Philosopher's Stone and is very rare. Fetch it out."

"*That*," I said, "is a dead body. *Your* dead body. Why don't *you* 'fetch it out'?"

Emrys laughed. "Because I am no longer a Keeper or a Holder, just a spirit, and a fading one at that."

"You've got a point," I admitted. I gingerly reached out, doing my best not to touch the exposed bones of the wrist. I eased my hand into the pocket and felt the stone inside, then pulled it out of the pocket. "It looks like flint."

"I suppose so," Emrys said. "To awaken the Board of the Earth, you must rub it with the stone."

"That's it?" I asked.

"It?" he cried. "Do you know how difficult it is finding a stone like that? I spent more than a hundred years searching before I found one!"

"A hundred years?" I asked. "What makes this stone so special?"

Emrys muttered something I didn't understand in tones that sounded suspiciously like curse words, and then said, "Just rub the stone on the Board, and you'll see."

I cradled the Board in my left arm and slowly rubbed the Philosopher's Stone over it. In my mind, I heard a low rumble, like the sound of a rockslide three valleys over, and then the Board suddenly changed. As I watched, one edge of the Board turned golden, and the color moved steadily across the entire surface until the entire thing was gold.

"Gold?" I whispered, awed.

"*That's* what makes the stone special, Keeper," Emrys said. "The Philosopher's Stone can turn one type of substance into another. In the case of certain metals and the wood of the Boards, it temporarily transmutes them into gold."

The transformation was brief and the Board quickly resumed its normal color of darkened wood. *"Emrys,"* a deep, rumbling voice said in my mind. *"Is that you at long last?"*

"No," I said. *"Emrys is long dead. I am the Keeper of the Boards, the Daughter of Destiny. I have come as the prophecy foretold."*

What seemed a really long time later, the Board spoke. *"I have no use for such things now, Keeper of the Boards. Shalizander the Creator has been dead for millennia, and the only person who has bothered me since was Emrys, a long time ago. Leave me to my sleep."*

"What?" I asked, stunned. *"Wake up! My will is your will. Our hungers are one and the same. Hear me and obey."*

Once again, there was silence.

"It doesn't want to wake up," I said to Emrys.

"The Board of the Earth is unlike the others, from what I understand," he said. "It is much more patient, and doesn't like the natural order of things to be disturbed. It has slept for a long time, so for the Board, *that* is now the natural order."

"Do you have any suggestions, then?"

"Use your will," he said. "I was only a Holder. I stole the Board from one of my father's agents. It allowed me to use some of its powers because it chose to at the time, not because I controlled it. *You* are the Keeper of the Boards, and if you provoke it hard enough, it will respond to you."

"I am the Keeper of the Boards," I repeated. *"The time of the prophecy has come. Already, I have the Board of the Winds, the Board of the Waters and the Board of the Flames."*

A faint groaning sound echoed in my mind. *"My brothers mean little to me. Their natures are transient and fickle, reveling in the fleeting destruction they may cause. Leave me to my long sleep, Keeper."*

"NO!" I shouted. *"If it takes until the end of time to wake you, I* will *wake you. I must—I don't have a choice. I . . . need you, if I am to make the Master Board of the Elements."*

"Need?" it asked. *"I have not been needed in a long time. Even Emrys did not* need *me."*

"I do," I said. *"Please."*

There was silence again, as if the Board was deliberating in its own, ponderous way. *"Has Emrys given you the key piece yet?"*

"No," I said.

"He cannot," the Board rumbled. *"He has never been one to appear weak, but if he had access to the key piece, we would not have rested here nearly so long. The key gives one the power of elemental binding, and with that, there is no natu-*

ral force that could stand against his might."

"Why can't he?" I asked.

"It is trapped on the other side of a magical field at the far end of this chamber. Morgan Le Fay was not satisfied to trap us with the closing of the portal. In the place Emrys had designated for the key, she built a magical trap. Once the key was placed there, the field sprang into existence. Neither Emrys nor I have the power to retrieve it."

"Well, that's good news," I said to Emrys.

"I take it he explained your second task," he said sourly.

"He mentioned it, yes," I said.

"Will you help me?" I asked the Board.

The response was a long time in coming. *"You have come to fulfill the prophecy of Shalizander the Creator?"*

"Yes."

"And you will retrieve the key piece and create the Master Board?"

"I will try," I said. *"That is all I can promise. I do not have the magical skills of Emrys, let alone Shalizander or Malkander."*

"That," it said, *"is unexpected. The line of Shalizander has always had magical talents."*

"Not me," I said. *"I'm just a regular girl trying to do a very irregular job. And keep my sanity at the same time."*

"My brothers disturb your rest?" it asked.

"Yes," I said. *"And they are very capricious. Sometimes they will help, sometimes not. They do*

not always answer questions in a way that makes sense."

"Such were the constraints put upon us by our creators," it said. *"Still, should I be joined with them, my influence should prove to . . . help in some of these matters."*

"You will awaken then?" I asked. *"And obey my word?"*

There was a low rumbling sound, not unlike a rockslide, and it said, *"Yes, Keeper, I will awaken and obey. Your will is my will."*

I let out a breath I didn't know I'd been holding. A sense of relief washed over me, and I felt my shoulder muscles relax a bit.

"It's awake," I said. "Though this Board seems different than the others, more . . . independent or something."

"In some ways, the Board of the Earth is more independent. It is certainly more reliable and steadier than the other Boards. However, do not be fooled into complacence. Just like the others, the Board has a will of its own and can become stubborn and unresponsive, more so than the others, should it choose to do so."

"I'll remember," I said, thinking that what I had really needed was an unpredictable Board. At least with the other three, I knew my distrust was well founded.

"Good," Emrys said. "Then your next task is upon you."

"The key piece," I said.

"Yes," he replied. "And I have no idea how you'll go about getting it. I tried for a very long time, and failed utterly."

"Show me," I said.

He moved to the far end of the chamber and I followed him, carrying the Board of the Earth with me. Buried among the crystal outcroppings was a small shelf of quartz. Rose-colored runes were etched along its edges and surface. The key piece, the small wooden object that I had seen in my dreams, was placed on the shelf. It was also rune-marked, with hundreds of tiny runes that were too small to distinguish in the dim light. They would probably require a jeweler's loupe to see properly.

Emrys frowned as he looked at it. "I have tried many spells to penetrate the magical shield that Morgan placed here." He pointed. "Look there. See that tiny rune? That is the only one I did not make. That one belongs to her, and I didn't see it until *after* I'd placed the key piece on the shelf. By then it was too late."

I leaned forward to get a better look at the rune. It was a small circle with an upside down arc meeting it on top. I was certain I'd seen it before, but couldn't remember where.

"What does the key piece do, exactly?" I asked.

"It binds the four Boards together," Emrys said. "It represents the fifth consistent element of our universe."

"Fifth element?" I asked. "What do you mean?"

Emrys sighed. "Didn't anyone teach you *anything* before you became the Keeper of the Boards?"

I narrowed my eyes and gave him my best dirty look.

"No," I said. "As a matter of fact, everyone died before they could share any information with me." *And some even torment me from beyond the grave.*

"I see," he said. "Very well then, a little education goes a long way. There are, as you know, four primary elements—earth, air, fire and water. These elements exist in various forms throughout our universe. Without them, there is no life. You understand this much, yes?"

I nodded. "Go on."

"The fifth element is more complex than that. The fifth element is *time*. Without time the elements cannot bind to create life. Without time, that life cannot perceive the elements—the building blocks of the universe. No matter how it may be marked or perceived, without time to bind them together, the elements themselves are meaningless."

I thought about it for a minute. "That makes sense, I suppose. But what does the key piece *do*? How does it work? Is it sentient like the other Boards?"

Emrys shook his head. "Not exactly. The key piece ties the others together and makes the creation of a Master Board possible. See how it's lower in the center? That's for the magic that will create the Board."

"But I saw you attach it to the Board of the Earth when you battled Coghlan."

"Yes," he said. "The key piece seems to make the Boards more powerful in some way."

"The key piece allows us to transcend time," the Board of the Earth rumbled.

"What do you mean?" I asked.

"With the key piece attached or the Master Board created, we can influence the elements in the present . . . or elsewhere in the time stream."

"Does Emrys know this?"

"Emrys was an excellent Holder, but he is not a Keeper. Some of the knowledge we possess is not to be given to those who are not Keepers."

"So you can change the past or the future?"

"Not precisely," it said. *"We can modify the elements elsewhere in the time stream. For example, we could create a river in a place where there hadn't been one, or put a mountain in a place where there isn't one now. However, our influence is limited to elements. We cannot change the outcomes of events as they relate to humans."*

"I'm not sure I understand."

"Time is not easily understood, Keeper. Think of it this way . . . Let us suppose that you wanted to save the life of someone who had died in a fire. We could, conceivably, modify the elements so that the fire never occurred—"

"So you could go back in time and save someone from death?"

"No. The fire would change, but some other

event would occur that would cause the death of that individual within the same approximate time. We are not permitted to change the outcome of human *events."*

"That doesn't do me a lot of good."

"Not yet," it said.

"Oh, wow," I said aloud. "That's . . . really something."

"What?" Emrys asked. "Did the Board tell you something you needed to know?"

"Yes, I think so," I said. "I don't know how it helps retrieve the key piece, but if what the Board has told me is the truth, the Master Board would be an artifact of unimaginable power in the right—or the wrong—hands."

"What did it say?" he demanded. "Tell me and I shall judge if it helps us or not."

"Do not reveal this to Emrys, Keeper," the Board of the Earth rumbled. *"His spirit still seeks a way to avoid permanent death and return to the land of the living. The knowledge is not applicable to retrieving the key piece."*

"I'm sorry, Emrys," I said. "But for now I think I will keep this information to myself."

"You would deny me?" he shouted. "After my long years of waiting to ensure that *you* could fulfill your destiny?"

"I would deny you," I said, "because you are wise enough to trust that the *Keeper* of the Boards should know a few things about the Boards that a *Holder* does not."

For a moment, he looked like he wanted to grab me and demand to know what I had been told, but then his shoulders slumped and he nodded in defeat.

"Very well. Still, you must retrieve the key piece."

"I *know* I've seen that symbol before," I said, looking at it again. "Do you know what it is?"

"Yes," he said. "It is a symbol from the science of astrology. The sign of the bull."

"That's where I've seen it!" I said. "In the newspaper. It's my zodiac sign!"

"Your sign?" he asked, incredulous. "You are a bull?"

"A Taurus," I said. "I was born on May eleventh."

"Is it possible . . ." he said, his words drifting off.

"What?" I asked.

"I believe that the magical field may not apply to you, Keeper," he said. "Somehow, Morgan Le Fay may have keyed the energy of the magic to you specifically. How she knew to do this, I do not know."

"What happens if you're wrong?" I asked. "And I touch the field?"

"Then you'll be here for a long time," he said.

"It will trap me?"

"No," he sighed. "It will kill you."

"How do you know that?" I asked.

His eyes blazed as he said, "What do you think killed me, you foolish child?"

"I was hoping old age," I admitted.

"No," he said. "The magic created by Morgan Le Fay is powerful enough to kill anyone not *meant* to touch the key piece."

Perfect, I thought. *What if I'm not the one?*

"She has apparently gone through some kind of . . . portal. There is no sign of her there."

"The Keeper isn't the kind to desert her allies. Wait for her to return and when she does, you'll have everything you seek."

"What if I'm not the one?" I asked. "What if all of this has been some kind of . . . freakish mistake?"

"I must admit that is possible," Emrys said. "But not probable."

"That's easy for you to say," I said. "You're already dead."

"Your fear is talking for you, Keeper," Emrys soothed. "It is highly unlikely that you could have recovered the other three Boards by accident or chance. You are the one meant to retrieve the key piece. And you have no choice but to try."

"No choice?" I asked. "I could always leave without it. Just take the Board of the Earth and go."

Emrys shook his head. "I tried that," he said. "The portal is closed, as you know. Without the key piece, the Board of the Earth cannot reopen it, and the other Boards cannot respond to your commands from this chamber. It is outside the realm of their influence."

I sighed, and then began laughing. The sound was one of utter despair and not a little amount of madness. I saw the concern on Emrys's face, and choked it off before I went into hysterics.

"Sorry," I said. "I was wondering why they'd been so quiet."

"So, as you now understand, you have little choice. Morgan was thorough, if nothing else. However, I believe you will succeed where I failed."

"I hope you're right," I said, resigning myself to attempting to break through the field. "I don't really want to spend the rest of eternity in here with you."

"Understandable," he said. "At this point, I'm less-than-great company."

"You are a master of understatement," I muttered, turning away from him to face the small alcove once more. Whatever magic was there was invisible. I couldn't see it or sense it, and had no way to know when I'd hit the field.

"Here goes nothing," I said, reaching out with my hand.

As my fingertips inched forward, I braced myself. Emrys hadn't said *how* the field reacted, but a massive lightning bolt wouldn't have been too much of a surprise. Just as my fingers passed over the rune, I felt something grab my hand, almost pulling me off my feet. I tried to yank my hand back, but it was too late. The magical field held me in place.

I yanked again, but nothing happened. Choosing a different route, I pushed forward and suddenly I could feel a gale force wind tearing at my skin. As I watched, I could see the skin actually folding in on itself and when I tried to make a fist, found it was impossible to do so—the force of the wind kept my fingers apart, the tendons shrieking as they were stretched far beyond normal limits.

"Keeper, I can tell you that the trap is elemental in nature. Trust in what you have become," the Board of the Earth said.

Even as my fingers stretched, I knew that this was the element of Air. These were winds that I could call and . . . I had nothing to fear from them. The winds stopped as suddenly as they started. I began to pull away, but was still held in place by the field.

A vague shimmering passed over the field and my hand was wet and cold. The liquid turned to ice and my skin took on the look—and feel—of frostbite. I couldn't move my fingers and my skin turned blue. The ache in my hand worked its way into my wrist and soon my teeth were chattering. Then I remember when I first acquired the Board of the Waters—and called ice and snow to cover my escape with Simon. Much like the winds, I could call this element, and it could not harm me. *Waters,* I thought, *and nothing more.* As fast as the thought crossed my mind, my hand was once again warm and dry.

Another shimmer passed across the field and then my hand began to burn. The skin charred and blackened as flames engulfed my hand and my nerves screamed with the pain. I pushed forward, trying to ignore the pain, knowing it wasn't real, couldn't be real. *This is fire,* I thought, *and I am the Keeper of the Flames.*

The flames flickered and died, and I felt the tension ease out of my straining shoulder muscles. I was panting with the exertion. Intellectually, I knew that all this was an illusion, part of the magical barrier I had to pass through to get the key piece. That didn't change how it felt to watch my hand freeze or burn. It *felt* real and it took all of my will to not scream and yank my arm until my hand fell off.

"Keep going, Keeper," the Board said. *"Only in passing the boundary layers will you obtain the key."*

I forced myself to push my hand deeper in the alcove. Slowly, it became heavier and heavier. My skin tone changed to the gray of granite and it felt as though my hand weighed a thousand pounds. I couldn't move it forward no matter how hard I pushed. A wave of exhaustion washed over me. *This is Earth,* I thought. *Heavy and slow and tired. I am like the Earth.*

"No," the Board said. *"You are the Keeper of the Earth. This is my element and I recognize its*

weight. Stop resisting, and let the energy pull you."

I did as the Board had suggested and the pressure immediately eased. My fingertips could almost touch the key piece. Freedom was a mere half-inch away. I eased my hand forward and then stopped as it grew wrinkled and liver-spotted. My nails grew long, curling in on themselves. My knuckles were swollen and bony, and just moving a finger hurt.

Time, I thought. *This is the element of time—and I am not its Keeper.*

The bones of my hands became more pronounced and the sensation of aging moved into my wrist. *It's going to age me until I'm dead,* I thought, beginning to panic.

"No, Keeper!" Emrys shouted. "One does not become the Keeper of Time!"

"Then what?" I screamed, even as the aging process continued up my arm. I wanted to yank my arm away, but I feared that in its brittle condition it would come right off.

"One recognizes that time transcends all elements," he said.

"Why?"

"Because it is the only element that is an illusion," he explained. "The only element created and measured by man!"

"What the hell does that mean?" I asked, even as the skin cracked and fell away from my hand to reveal yellowed bones.

"It means that *you* control your perception of time," he said.

It all clicked. That was why some days lasted forever and others went by in a blink. Time, like beauty, was in the eye of the beholder. *Time,* I realized, *was mine to perceive.* I looked at my hand, my arm and saw them as they truly were, and the illusion of age passed away. The resistance of the magical field was gone and I almost fell as my hand shot forward.

My fingertips brushed the key piece and I clutched it in my hand.

"Well done!" Emrys said.

I pulled the key piece from the alcove and looked at it. "Thank you."

"You should wait to attach it to the Boards until you reach your final task," Emrys said. "I suspect it sits directly in the center of the four Boards."

His voice sounded different, weaker, and as I looked closer, I saw him slowly fading away.

"Final task?" I asked.

"You must release the phoenix from its stone prison within the cube," Emrys said, "and then create the Master Board."

"How do I do that?" I asked. "And where are you going?"

"I am released, Keeper," he shouted, his voice filled with joy. "And I go to whatever awaits me, finally, in the next world."

"Wait! How do I release the phoenix?" I cried. "How do I make the Master Board awaken?"

"Add the Board of the Earth to the other three and place them on the altar." His voice was barely audible. "Put the ashes of the phoenix in the bowl and call upon its element. The Master Board will be formed."

"Where am I going to get the ashes of a phoenix?" I asked, thinking that it had taken him a hundred years to find the one thing that would awaken the Board of the Earth.

"Silly child," he said, now almost invisible. "What do you think the binding element of the stone you brought here is made of?"

Then, just as I thought he was completely gone, his form grew more solid again. "One last word, Keeper of the Boards," he said. "My father was Malkander, also a Creator of the Boards. He knows magics that far exceed Shalizander's greatest ambitions and your worst nightmares. Be wary of him and all his heirs."

There was a flicker of light, and then the spirit of Emrys was gone.

I sighed, wishing that I'd had more time to ask questions. It never failed that when a good source of information availed itself to me, I wasn't able to take full advantage of it.

"How long have I slept, Keeper?" the Board of the Earth asked. *"It seems quite some time."*

"A very long time," I said.

"And my brothers?"

"As long or longer," I said. *"They wait for us above."*

"Good," it replied. *"You may be sure that my influence will help steady them."*

"I certainly hope so," I said.

I walked back to the short passage and remembered that the portal was gone.

"How do I open the portal?" I asked the Board.

"Attach the key piece to me, and will it to exist."

I pulled the key piece out of my jacket pocket and held it up to the Board, then clicked it into place. Then, I focused my will on the place where the portal had been, willing it to open here and now. A surge of energy passed through the Board, unlike anything I had previously felt, and I watched as green ribbons of energy slowly formed, and then yellow, and finally, they mixed together and were blue.

The portal was ready. And I was more than ready for the night to be over, though a part of me wondered, as I stepped through the portal, if all of this had been a bit too easy. Morgan's trap had made it impossible for anyone but me to get the key piece, but even then, it hadn't been the worst danger I had faced.

I stepped through the portal, and on the other side, with the flare of lights once again coloring my vision, it became immediately clear that "too easy" was a bit of an understatement. A bonfire had been lit near the base of the altar, and a large group of men—all dressed in the same dark clothing, almost a uniform—now surrounded the inner circle of stones. Their faces were completely concealed, other than their eyes, and all of them were armed.

Both Armand and Simon had several men near each of them.

I rubbed my eyes, and tried not to panic. The other Boards were still on the central altar.

"Jenna," Simon said, sounding relieved. "I hoped you were okay."

I nodded, and said, "I'm fine. What's going on here?"

A tall man stepped through the ring of stones. "Ahh," he said when he saw me. "Our last guest has arrived." His voice wasn't familiar, but it had an accent similar to Simon's.

"Who are you?" I demanded.

"I'm sure your friend Simon would like to explain," he said. "I'd hate to deprive him of the pleasure—it might be the last moment of pedantic fun he ever has."

I turned to Simon, and he sighed. "Long ago, there was a secret sect within the Vatican. They were referred to as the Shadows of God, or sometimes just the Vatican Shadows. For hundreds of years, they did the Church's truly dirty work—espionage, assassination, theft."

"Very Christian," I said. "Right in line with the commandments."

Simon frowned. "I believed, as did Armand, that they had long since been disbanded. There has been no evidence of their activity in many long years, and many of them were corrupt, so the Holy See had a good reason to send them packing.

Unlike the Templar Knights, the Vatican Shadows were a force for evil, rather than good."

"And there's been no sign of them until . . ."

"Until those two men broke into your room in Scotland," he answered. "I'm sorry, Jenna. I'd hoped I was mistaken."

"The wolves from my dream," I said. "They are the wolves."

"An apt description, Ms. Solitaire. And as you no doubt know from your dreams, wolves are predators and we hunt in packs," the leader said. "This hunt is all but over, I think. You will assemble the Master Board of the Elements or I will kill your friend Armand. Should this not prove sufficient motivation, I will then kill Simon Monk."

Even as the words left his mouth, I saw that he felt surprised at what he'd said—almost as though what he'd said in his mind and the words that came out were different. I wondered if he'd say something else, but he gave a minute shake of his head and a look of resolve came into his eyes.

"Do it now," he ordered.

I looked at the men surrounding us and knew that even if I called on the Boards' magic, Simon or Armand, and maybe both, would be dead before I could use it on all of them. These men were *not* like Peraud, who had been constrained from truly harming me for reasons I had never understood. And I had no doubt that they wouldn't hesitate to kill if they even suspected that I wasn't going to do as I'd been told.

"All right," I said to the leader. I was already tired, but I didn't have a choice.

I walked to the altar and connected the Board of the Earth to the other three Boards. The yellow lines that had previously appeared on the altar flowed around this new shape, once again outlining the Boards in their new configuration. In their midst, I placed the key piece, then stepped back and waited.

When nothing happened, the leader said, "What's going on? Something should be happening!" Once again, he appeared surprised at his own words.

"This isn't like pulling a rabbit out of a hat," I snapped. "In order to activate it, I need the ashes of a phoenix."

"The ashes of a phoenix? The mythical bird?" he said. Now the tone of his voice had changed, sounding older than before. "How is that possible?"

I sighed, even as a plan began to form in my head. It would be dangerous, but it might be our only hope of getting out of this alive. I knew that once they had the Master Board, they'd kill us all. I also suspected that something or someone else was somehow controlling what the leader of the Vatican Shadows was doing and saying.

I looked at him and shrugged, trying to maintain a casual pose. "There's only one way."

"Then do it," he grated. Beneath his mask, I saw the man's jaw muscles tense as he tried to control himself.

I called on the Board of the Flames. *"I am the Keeper of the Boards,"* I said. *"My will is your will, our hungers are one."*

It responded in the voice of a blazing bonfire. *"What is your will, Keeper?"*

I knelt to open my backpack, removed the phoenix stone, and set it atop the Boards themselves. The glowing lines changed from yellow to red. *"I had a vision, a dream, of three gigantic fire elementals. Do such beings exist?"*

"Deep in the bowels of the Earth, Keeper," it said. *"They frolic among fires that no man has ever seen, except in nightmares."*

"I wish you to summon one forth. Here and now, and have it dance atop the phoenix stone."

It laughed, and there was a malicious glee in its tone that sent a chill down my spine. *"As you will, Keeper,"* it said.

I felt a massive surge of energy pulse from the Board, down through the altar stone and into the ground itself. Beneath our feet, the ground actually thrummed, like an electric current ran through it.

"What are you doing?" the man demanded.

I turned to him and smiled grimly. "I am the Keeper of the Boards. Ashes can only come from one place." Beneath our feet, the ground actually shuddered and several of the massive stones around us shifted in their place.

The Vatican Shadows looked around wildly, and the man took a step toward me, even as I moved closer to the altar stone. "What's going on?" he cried. "What are you talking about?"

At my feet, the ground cracked open. Steam roses in jets and the first glimmers of orange and yellow and crimson flickered into the night.

"The elemental comes, Keeper," the Board of the Flames said. *"Prepare yourself."*

"The only place they can," I said to him, as his eyes widened in fear.

A massive creature of crimson flames burst from the ground and leaped into the air. It was a perfect match for the fire elementals of my dreams. Red and yellow flames flickered around its huge, vaguely humanoid form, which burned so hot that the temperature in the inner circle of stones skyrocketed. Fists of magma and eyes of coal made the elemental seem like a creature summoned straight from the depths of Hell. And it was.

"Ashes," I shouted, "come from fire!"

Above us, the gigantic elemental plunged downward, its voice roaring, and headed straight for the altar, the phoenix stone, the Boards . . . and me.

"She's summoned some sort of fire elemental! My men will all die and she'll escape! What kind of sorceress is she?"

"Control yourself! Is the elemental attacking your men?"

"No . . . I don't believe so . . ."

"Then be patient. Now is not the time to lose your nerve. Wait and see . . ."

The fire elemental slammed into the altar stone like a burning, whirling tornado. Flames blossomed in the inner ring of stones, and I heard screams of pain and terror as men dove for cover. As I had expected, both Simon and Armand used the amazing distraction to try and break free of their guards.

I stood in the center of the inferno, untouched, protected by the power of the Boards. I felt unusually calm, though the scene was an eerie reminder of my dreams back in Pompeii, when the fire elementals had consumed me even as the spiteful Boards had left me to my fate.

But this was different. The Boards had not deserted me and there was only one fire elemental, not three. And I was not alone.

"Guard your will, Keeper!" the Board of the Winds said. *"We may summon elementals, but it is* you *who must control them!"*

The words were no sooner uttered than I felt a searing pain on my wrist as I was nearly yanked off my feet. I looked down and saw that the elemental had grabbed my arm, and its smoky voice rumbled in my head. *"Dance with me, summoner, and feel the consuming sting of my touch."*

I yanked my arm away.

"I am not a mere summoner," I said. *"I am the Keeper of the Boards and you will bend to my will."*

I felt its laughter as much as heard it.

"I bow to no one, 'Keeper of the Boards'," it said.

"You will to me," I replied. *"There shall be no dance. You will burn the phoenix stone to ash, then return from where you came."*

It leaped into the air, spinning, and flames shot out in all directions. Around me, several of the Vatican Shadows rolled around in agony, trying to extinguish their flaming clothes and hair. Simon and Armand had curled into fetal positions and appeared to be almost digging into the ground to escape.

"Never!" it cried. *"I am free from my fiery prison and I will now make this world my home. There will be a great burning in this land such as has never been seen before!"*

"No!" I said, pouring all of my mental strength

into the command. *"You will do as I have said and no more."*

The elemental spun faster, and flames shot higher into the night sky.

"Keeper, I can summon its opposite number, a water elemental to give it battle," the Board of the Waters said. *"It will grant us time to leave this place."*

"No," I said, trying to stay focused on the elemental. I called out to the Board of the Flames. *"Help me!"*

It laughed, and the gleeful sound was much like the elemental's voice.

"Prove yourself worthy of the title, Keeper," it roared, laughing harder. *"Control the elemental or turn it loose to wreak havoc on the countryside!"*

Once again, the elemental plunged down toward the altar stone, spinning and whirling, as flames exploded in all directions, wreathing Stonehenge in a ring of fire.

"You have been summoned to perform a task, creature of fire," I said. *"You. Will. Do. As. I. Command. NOW!"*

I concentrated all the force of my will into the command, every ounce of energy I had into trying to subdue the living flame before me.

I felt the elemental resist, pushing its willpower against mine. I sensed that it wasn't very intelligent, and that its wants were primal and simple, tied to its nature. It struggled fiercely and I visualized a series of unbreakable metal bands surrounding it, forcing it down to the altar stone.

"No!" it said. *"You cannot make me!"*

"I can and I do," I said, my teeth gritted.

All around me, the superheated air scorched lungs and singed hair. I knew if I didn't contain it, everyone here would die. I pushed harder still, and felt all the muscles in my body lock with the strain.

"You. Will. Do. As. I. Command," I repeated.

Suddenly, it was as though a cord had snapped, and I felt the tension ease.

"I . . . will do as you command," it said, its voice now sullen, like a scolded child. In no small way, I was again reminded of the Board of the Flames.

The elemental lowered itself to the phoenix stone, and a new wave of fire and heat burst from it, this time focused on the altar. In the heart of the flames, I saw the phoenix stone melt, coming apart in tiny fragments, which dropped into the bowl in the center of the connected Boards.

I kept my will focused until the final pieces of the phoenix stone liquefied into the bowl. A sudden burst of light flared in the center, and an entity separate from the elemental burst into the night sky, trailing beautiful streams of fire behind it until it flickered and disappeared.

A wave of exhaustion rocked me, and I knew I was reaching the limits of my endurance.

"Return to whatever fire spawned you," I ordered the elemental.

"Yes . . . summoner." Slowly, it lowered itself from the altar stone and I watched as it crawled

back into the ground, pulling the earth down on top of itself. There was a final, disgruntled rumble, followed by one last wave of heat, and then it was gone.

I staggered, and turned back to the altar. Where the four Boards had once been, there was now a much smaller object, about the size of a salad plate, that looked like the star symbol of chaos. Nine points radiated outward from a center marked with hundreds of tiny runes. I realized that the Master Board had been created, and wanted to touch it, to hold it in my hands, but the exertion to control the elemental had proved too much and I slumped, half-conscious, against the altar stone.

I closed my eyes for a moment, and listened to the sound of the night returning, men groaning in pain and fear as they climbed back to their feet.

I sensed a presence nearby, and opened my eyes to see the leader of the Vatican Shadows, his facemask burned away, along with most of his hair, and heat blisters rising on his mottled face. His eyes were dark and angry, and he moved with the slow caution of someone whose whole body hurt. He nudged me with his boot, and said, "Well done, Keeper of the Boards. It's too bad it nearly killed you. That is going to ruin all the fun I had planned for tonight."

I knew what he was about to do, and it crossed my mind to warn him, but I kept my mouth shut. There was something about the Boards that brought out the worst in people: greed, anger, fear, hate—all those emotions seemed much more concentrated whenever they were near, and it was clear that he was being influenced by them as well as by whatever other entity was controlling him.

He picked up the Master Board with both hands. Everyone still alive in the circled stones watched in awed silence as he lifted it over his head in triumph. For a single moment, he held the power of all the elements in his hands, and then he staggered and let out the most piercing scream of agony I had ever heard.

I saw Simon and Armand draw back in horrified shock as they watched.

The man's arms shook as he tried to throw the Master Board away, but it stuck to his hands as though glued to them.

Without a single mental command from me, it drained every ounce of water out of his body, and still he shrieked, all of the liquid consumed from within, and making him look like a living mummy. He fell to his knees and burst into flame. His clothing, skin, boots, everything flared white-hot for a millisecond, and as his final screech of agony rent the air, he disintegrated into a pile of glowing ash. A brief, cold wind passed through the stones, and his remains were swept into the air and gone. Like he had never existed at all.

On the ground where he had stood, the center of the Master Board glowed with power, pulsed, and then darkened to the scorched wood hues that were the same on every Board.

"Now!" Armand cried out, as he turned on his stunned guards.

Simon did the same thing and out of the darkness surrounding us, I saw about a dozen men appear. I had figured that Armand must have had reinforcements nearby—it seemed he never traveled without them.

Several of the Vatican Shadows pulled their guns,, but no one was able to fire before the Templars swarmed in. The combat was too close for anyone to shoot at random, and the grunts of bodies impacting each other grew louder as everyone used hand-to-hand techniques to break bones; throw opponents to the ground, and knock each other unconscious, or worse.

My entire body aching, I somehow got to my hands and knees and crawled toward the Master Board. All around me, people fought and cursed, and I heard the dull, wet thuds of fists against muscle and bone. I glanced up and saw Armand and Simon fighting back to back—Simon with his fists and Armand with magic in the shape of softball-sized globes of fire and ice.

I crawled forward, and looked again. They seemed to be giving a good account of themselves, but even counting the reinforcements, they were surrounded by at least five men, and it was only going to be a matter of time until they were overwhelmed.

I reached the Master Board, ducking as a black-clad Vatican Shadow flew over my shoulder and rolled away to continue fighting his opponent, a blond-haired younger man whose right shoulder bore the familiar insignia of the Templar Knights.

I stretched out my hand, hoping that it wouldn't do the same to me as it had to the Vatican Shadow, hoping for peace. My outstretched fingers had nearly grasped it when Shalizander screamed a warning.

"The phoenix!" she cried. *"It returns!"*

I looked up at the night sky and saw a fiery, winged comet heading straight for us.

Through the melee, I saw Armand go to his knees, and then a vicious blow knocked him on his back. He didn't move, and I assumed he was unconscious. Several of the Vatican Shadows now closed on Simon, who began backing away.

I called out to the Boards, and the slow, rumbling voice of the Board of the Earth answered. *"Do you require protection, Keeper, for that is my purpose?"*

"Yes!"

The ground began to shake and rumble and I watched, amazed, as several large stone figures pulled themselves free of the soil. They stood nearly seven feet tall, with broad shoulders and heavy legs that looked like stacked boulders.

"Stone golems, Keeper," the Board of the Earth said. *"They are often used as guardians of sacred places such as this."*

They moved quickly for such heavy beings, and I saw one lash out with a curled fist, knocking one of the Vatican Shadows clear across the clearing, and into one of the stone monoliths surrounding us. From the crack of his body hitting the stone, I knew he'd never get up again. Another golem grasped two men by the back of the neck and slammed them together like a pair of human tambourines. They slumped to the ground and didn't move.

The sky above Stonehenge lit up in a brilliant, fiery rainbow as the phoenix came down. Its cry was an eerie screech that sent a shiver down my back and made me clench my teeth. The noise was that of long nails being run down a chalkboard.

"Simon," I yelled, somehow finding the strength to wave my arms. "Get out of there!"

Those still on their feet were trapped, as the stone golems laid low any who came within their reach, and before they could escape, the phoenix was among them. Screams of agony were cut short as men became human torches, burning alive even as they tried to flee the majestic, flaming creature of myth.

It swooped down among them, and every living being it touched with its outstretched wings died in seconds. The smell was horrendous, with the reek of blackened flesh and charred hair everywhere.

I looked for Simon again and saw him duck past one attacker. His right eye was nearly swollen shut and his clothing smoked. A Vatican Shadow jumped in front of him and Simon kicked the man where it counted, then clubbed him on the back of the head with both fists as he went down. He jumped over him and kept coming toward me.

I knew if I could reach out and control the Master Board, I could call off the phoenix and save whoever still lived in the conflagration.

"Bring the golems closer to me," I ordered the Board of the Earth. *"Tell them only to attack those who threaten myself or Simon."*

"As you will, Keeper." I felt a thrum of power and the golems lumbered in my direction, their heavy steps shaking the ground.

On the far side of the stone ring, several Templars banded together and raced through the chaos and the flames to reach Armand. One of them picked him up in a fireman's carry and the other two guarded his retreat to the far side of the stone ring. I couldn't tell if he had been more severely injured during his time on the ground.

"Daughter," Shalizander said. *"You must reach the Master Board and quickly, before someone else does!"*

"Oh, shut up." Still, I inched closer to where the Board lay on the ground, hoping that the current brawlers would overlook me and focus on the more immediate threats—like the golems and the phoenix.

Fire was everywhere, crisping the grass and flickering against the stones as the phoenix roared through the area once more. I peered around for

Simon, saw him wave back two of Armand's men and keep moving toward me.

"Tell the golems to let him through!" I ordered the Board of the Earth.

"As you will, Keeper," it replied.

Simon leaped over one last assailant and then rolled past the feet of one of the golems. I held out a hand for him and he looked up at me from the ground and grinned. Then he took my hand and I helped him to his feet. His cheeks were smudged with ash, and his eye was already turning black and blue. He pulled me into his arms, so close I felt his racing pulse.

I just held him, exhausted and aching, and yet somehow feeling safe. I knew that together there was no challenge we couldn't face, and if we couldn't be together as more than friends right now, the future was still ahead of us.

"Jenna," he said, his calm, confident voice already reassuring me. "Are you all right?"

"Tired," I said, finally relaxing. "Really tired."

"Just lean into me," he whispered. "Can you make the phoenix go away before it fries us to cinders?"

"I don't know," I admitted. "I haven't even touched the Master Board yet."

"Daughter . . . Jenna," Shalizander said, *"you must focus. Pick up the Master Board and then you will be able to dismiss the phoenix."*

"Ideas?" Simon said.

Over his shoulder, I saw one of the golems thump a man in the head who came too close.

"I need to get the Master Board," I said. "I think that will allow me to control the phoenix."

"Where is it?" Keeping me clasped in his arms, he slowly turned us around, so he could scan the ground.

"It's right there," I said, moving him so that we could both see it. "But I don't know if I even have the strength to control it. What if it's like the Board of the Winds and tries to control me? Or like the Board of the Flames and fights me with everything its got? I'm already pretty beat."

"I know," he said, "but didn't Emrys say that once you had the Master Board, many of those difficulties would go away?"

I nodded, not wanting to let go of him. Overhead, the phoenix flew in wide circles, and there was very little movement around the stones as everyone had run away or died in the fight or the fires. Flames flickered here and there on still-smoldering bodies. It was obviously looking for another target.

I sighed, knowing that he and Shalizander were right. It was time to pick up the Master Board and make it mine, and being tired was a lousy excuse for letting more people get hurt.

"All right," I said, starting to step away from him.

Simon's body stiffened against me, and without warning he spun me completely around at the same time as he cried, "Look out!"

He staggered against me, and suddenly I was

holding him up. There was an odd look in his eyes, and his expression was one I'd never seen cross his face before. I looked down and saw that the front of his shirt was wet. Without thinking about it, I put my hand to his chest, feeling warm wetness there. When I pulled it away and held it up to see by the nearby flames, my hand was red with his blood.

Simon sagged in my arms, and it was like everything in the world just went away. I couldn't hear or see anything else but him. I lowered him to the ground, and felt a sense of confusion wash over me. What had happened?

His hands fluttered weakly at his sides and I ripped open his shirt to look at the wound. Everything became clear. I hadn't heard the gunfire, but someone had tried to shoot me. Simon had whirled me around, and the bullet . . .

My thoughts were jumbled. *Simon's been shot. I didn't hear gunfire.*

His blood was on my hands, my clothes.

He coughed, and the sound was wet and raspy.

Simon's chest was covered in blood, and it was leaking out of the hole in his sternum. It was leaking so fast. The bullet must have gone through his body. Why didn't it hit me?

I wadded up the torn pieces of his shirt and put it over the wound.

Where is Armand? I wondered. *Where is the Board?*

Simon spasmed, his legs kicked weakly. He was trying to say something.

Overhead, the phoenix called out once more.

I looked at my own chest, and saw blood there, but none of it was mine. Where did the bullet go?

"Simon?" I said, leaning down and putting my ear to his mouth. "Simon?"

"He did what he was meant to do, daughter," Shalizander's voice said, her tone telling me that she *approved* of what Simon had done. *"He protected you."*

Sound and motion returned to the world, and everything sped up again.

My emotions caught up with me and the red in my vision wasn't from the fires.

It was rage.

"I used a Rite of Command to have your man pick up the Board . . ."

"You fool! He was destroyed instantly, yes?"

"Yes, and now a melee has broken out. Armand is smarter than I thought. He brought reinforcements."

"Of course he did. He's *not stupid."*

"I don't think I like your tone."

"I don't care what you like or don't like at the moment. What's important is that the Boards and the Keeper are recovered—at any cost."

Time stood still, sped up, and slowed once more. Sounds—like the horrid screech of the phoenix or the yells of men fighting and dying—ceased to have real meaning. Simon had been shot, he was bleeding to death in my arms, and we were miles away from the nearest hospital.

He was going to die unless I saved him. And I had no way to do so. I didn't have any magic, and the Boards would be no help. Several more gunshots rang out and I heard a sharp buzzing as a bullet blurred past my ear. I ignored it. Simon was dying, and he was all I could see at the moment.

I felt the muscles in my jaw clench, and my stomach roiled, as though I was going to be sick. I swallowed and opened my mouth to say something, anything, but all that came out was an anguished scream.

"Shalizander!" I cried in my mind. *"Help him!"*

Shalizander's voice was as calm as ever. *"I can help him, perhaps—but only if you complete the ritual."*

Simon had told me never to do it. I had promised myself that I wouldn't. Malizander had warned me that this day might come.

Simon was dying.

I looked down at his pale face, the pain etched into his features, the flow of blood still leaking, more slowly now, from his chest. It was necessary, but Shalizander was going to get more than she'd bargained for.

I pulled my pack off the ground and a detached part of my mind noticed that it had been burned in several places, and the leather was melted in others. I yanked on the zipper and when it stuck, I tore the pack open. The dagger was inside, still in its sheath.

I pulled it free and sent a mental command to the Board of the Earth, *"Tell the golems they are to kill anyone who approaches that is not a Templar knight."*

"It will be done, Keeper," the Board replied.

I lay down on the ground and pulled the dagger from the sheath. *"I'm coming for you, Shalizander."*

"Then come, my daughter, and let us see who is the stronger."

Lifting the dagger as far away from my chest as I could, I took a deep breath, and prayed that Simon could hold on for just a while longer. Then I plunged it straight down, as hard as I could, into my heart.

The pain was blinding, an icy cold wave that passed through me. I felt the cold metal buried in my chest, my heart struggling to beat around it. Once, twice. Again.

My legs thrashed and kicked and faintly, I heard the scream of the phoenix. It felt that I was dying.

Another wave of ice passed over me. Then heat, like the burn of the fire elemental.

My heart thudded once more, and I felt a draining sensation as the dagger sucked away my life force.

One beat. Another. Sharp, agonizing pain as the muscle constricted around the blade.

Then nothing.

I couldn't take a breath, my vision clouded, sound faded, faded, and then . . .

Darkness.

Time passes. A second. A minute. Hours? Days? I do not know. In the darkness of the void between worlds, it is impossible to tell.

I cannot see or hear or feel for what seems a long time. I think I have failed, that all I have done is ensured Simon's death and my own. How can this be? I wonder. I did not miss my heart, the blade struck true. What has gone wrong?

Then I know. I can think. My grandfather's words from long ago come back to me, and I hear them in my mind. "Jenna, the reason most people fail is because they are afraid. Afraid to try. Afraid to succeed. Afraid to fail. It's a form of mental paralysis that projects defeat before the battle has even been fought. As long as you can think, you must never be afraid. Your mind will always be your greatest weapon."

I can think. This darkness is not natural. It is a creation of Shalizander—her first step in our battle. I focus my will on the darkness. This, I say, is an illusion, a cheap parlor trick that frightens me into inaction.

I will *see past it.*

The darkness parts like a curtain, and I am in the Tower again.

Peraud hangs from his chains, a man and a spirit broken on Shalizander's rack. Yet . . . his eyes burn. He knows I am here to fight.

Shalizander rises from her seat near the window.

"I wondered," she says, "if you could see your way past the darkness. Welcome, my daughter." She gestures around the room as though I have never been here before, as though she is a hostess welcoming a guest.

"I told you before to stop calling me that." There is a faint copper taste in my mouth, and I realize it is blood. My blood. I spit on the floor and Shalizander raises an eyebrow.

"How . . . unbecoming," she says. "Your manners are failing you, just like your body is failing you in the real world."

Ignoring her, I spit again as blood fills my mouth. I am not a physical form, yet I bleed. How . . . ?

Illusion, I remind myself, is her first weapon of choice. The blood is not real. I spit again and the taste is gone. "Nice try," I say. "But you'll have to do better than petty tricks."

"This place," Shalizander says, "is beyond the boundaries of time. It is a construct of my magic and my will. In this place, I am *all laws—natural, metaphysical, or otherwise. You cannot beat me here, daughter. Even the Boards have no power in this place."*

I step closer to her.

"I don't need the Boards," I say. "I have my will, and this charade has gone on long enough. You will surrender your powers to me, allowing me free use of them for so long as I am the Daughter of Destiny, or so help me God . . ."

Shalizander laughs. "You'll what?" she asks. "You'll do nothing! You can do nothing to me here. The only magics that work here are mine. Isn't that right, Peraud?"

Peraud raises his head and nods weakly. "She

speaks the truth. No magics work in this place but hers."

"I don't have any magics of my own anyway," I say.

"But," Peraud continues as though I haven't spoken, "there are always other . . . ways." His eyes once more catch mine, and the desperation I see in them is equal to the power and madness I saw in them on the slopes of Mount Vesuvius.

"He keeps trying," Shalizander says. "It's endearing, in a way."

She shakes her head and turns back to me. "No, my daughter. It is not I *who will surrender. It is* you. *You will give up this foolish notion of using my powers and allow me willing access to your mind and your body so that the Boards can be gathered together again and my destiny fulfilled."*

I continue to look at Peraud and he silently mouths three words. "Kick. Her. Ass."

His meaning comes clear, and I find myself strangely reminded of Simon, of his fierce strength in the face of overwhelming odds. I turn back to Shalizander. I feel the nasty grin rise on my face, and try to hide it. I step closer to her.

"You're wrong," I say. "It's not your destiny. It's mine!"

Then I punch her in the face as hard as I can.

I feel her nose bone crack beneath my knuckles and Shalizander reels backward, her hands flying to her face. Blood pours from her nose and seeps through her fingers.

"Again!" Peraud says. "Strike before she recovers!"

I step closer, my fist raised, and then stop. I shake my head.

"No," I say. "I'm not a schoolyard bully. My grandfather would be ashamed."

Her hands muffle her voice, but I can clearly make out her words. "You ungrateful child."

"I don't owe you anything," I say. "You haven't given me a gift, Shalizander. You and your damn Boards have taken everything *from me."*

"Too late," Peraud mutters, his voice tired and broken once again.

A long, silent moment passes, then she straightens and her hands drop away from her face. I see that it is completely healed. She stares at me and in her gaze I feel her anger, her powers, her strength. She has existed for so long, feeding on her hate, that nothing else exists for her but her own vision. She sighs and says, "Jenna, I haven't taken everything from you . . . but I will!"

Her arm pulls back and I see the globe of fire in her palm. It streaks toward me and hits me in the chest. I'm certain I will be burned alive, but the fiery orb crackles once and then goes out.

"What is this?" she cries. "There is no magic here but mine!"

Once more, she throws a fireball, and it fails. She tries ice, and that strikes me too, but does no damage. She summons a massive lightning bolt and hurls it at me with all her strength. It ricochets away and dissipates into the floor. Again and again, she tries and nothing harms me.

I am as incredulous as she is, with no explanation as to how I am untouched.

"You are the Daughter of Destiny," *a new voice says in my mind.* "There shall be no deviation from the prophecy."

A wave of confidence washes over me. Shalizander is trapped by her own prophetic vision. Whatever forces in the universe control such things, they clearly do not intend to allow someone to change it—not even the person who uttered the words.

The voice says no more, but Shalizander does not give up. Instead, she chooses a new tactic. I feel a pressure in my mind, a weight squeezing down on my thoughts. I turn my focus inward, as though I want to communicate with the Boards, and I can sense the strength of Shalizander's will.

It presses down on me, harder and harder.

The words, "Surrender. Surrender. Surrender," pound in my head, throbbing like a drum.

I press back against her with my own chant, "Never. Never. Never."

The pressure builds, and I'm forced to close my eyes, block all my thoughts except one. "Never."

"Surrender."

"Never."

"SURRENDER!"

"NEVER!"

"YOU MUST SURRENDER!"

My mental scream is so loud that I wonder if I have shattered my own eardrums.

"I. WILL. NEVER. GIVE. IN. TO. YOU!"

Shalizander screams, too, and the pressure relents.

I open my eyes and across the room, my ultimate ancestor stares at me. She is holding her head in her hands and tears run down her face.

"I will never give in to you, Shalizander," I say. "You must surrender to me."

"Your will is strong, Jenna," she says. "Stronger than I expected."

"It has to be," I say. "I have been given no other choice."

"I am not beaten," she says. "Somehow . . . you should not be immune to my powers here."

"But I am," I say. "I am the Daughter of Destiny."

"You need my magic," Shalizander says. "You can't argue with that because it's truth. The stakes grow larger every day."

"And you need me," I say. "If I refuse, Malkander's prophecy wins."

"Then there is no other choice," she admits. "We must work together."

Peraud moans in despair from the other side of the room. I am his only hope of escape from this place, and that hope is now gone.

"Will you release him?" I ask.

She knows whom I am speaking of. "No," she says. "And don't think of trying. One person cannot undo another's spell while that caster lives in any form. It is the first rule of magic, and one you will learn to abide by."

"Very well," I say. "We will work together."

"You will have to let me in," she says, "to use my powers."

"I know. But should you try to take control of me, I will banish you back to this Tower and I will not take one additional step toward recovering the rest of the Boards. Agreed?"

She sighs and nods. "Agreed."

"Good," I say. "Now I have to get back and save Simon. How do I return to my body and not die of the wound inflicted by the dagger?"

"I will send you," she says. "But there is one other thing, Jenna."

"What's that?" I ask.

"The contest between us has just begun. You have barely touched on the strength of the Boards, and you are not fit to fill my worst apprentice's shoes in magic. In that arena, only I can be the master between us. You will learn, or I will devote all my energy and considerable powers to finding a way to break you. Do you understand?"

Between the lines, she is saying that this contest isn't finished yet, and that she's agreed to what is necessary . . . for now.

"I understand, Shalizander," I say. "But you understand something, too. I won't compromise my values for the sake of expedience."

Shalizander laughs. "You are the Keeper of the Boards, Jenna. In time, your so-called values will have no meaning to you, except those that further your agenda."

"We'll see," I say.

"We already have." She chuckles. "Or have you already forgotten those two men you had killed in Scotland?"

I shake my head. "I was protecting myself."

Shalizander's smile is tight and icy cold. "You destroyed your enemies using the power of the Boards—it doesn't matter what terms you want to couch it in, it's all the same. And I haven't even mentioned poor Peraud here—it must have been something to feel his life drain away as you plunged that dagger into his chest—"

"You will take me back right now!"

"Then go," she says. "And begin to learn what real magic can and cannot do."

She waves her hand and I feel myself float up into the void. Her voice follows me and I feel a trickle of fear. ". . . what real magic can and cannot do."

The void is cold and silent. I shudder and open my eyes to . . .

Four men with the insignia of Templar Knights on their shoulders look down at me, concern etched on their faces. The dagger was still in my chest. My heart was not beating.

"Remove the dagger and your heart will resume beating," Shalizander's voice said.

I grasped the hilt of the dagger in my right hand. I heard gasps, and one of the Templars yelled when I moved. I yanked on it, and the pain was excruciating. The blade scraped against my sternum, snagged, and finally came loose.

I screamed in agony as it left my body, along with the last ounces of oxygen left in my lungs as waves of ice and fire washed over me. I plunged the dagger into the ground at my side. My heart beat, a lurching, ungainly rhythm. My lungs hitched and convulsed as they tried to draw air into my body. I gasped once, twice, and then finally drew a normal breath.

My sternum bone shifted and popped as it knitted itself together, as my gaze fell on the Templars hovering over me. Their faces were pale with shock. I'm certain they believed me dead.

"Help me up," I said, and when they hesitated, I added, "Now."

Two of them found the courage to reach out and grasp my arms, and helped me to my feet.

"How long have I been out?" I asked.

One of them, the younger, blond man I'd seen in the midst of the fighting earlier, answered. "Just a few minutes. We saw you . . . we saw what happened and brought Armand over here behind those creatures."

I saw Armand lying on the ground behind me, the golems standing patient guard over those few of us who had survived the confrontation. His breathing was steady and regular, and I breathed a sigh of relief. He'd just been knocked silly.

Simon, on the other hand, was deathly pale. His breathing was so shallow that I had to watch him for several long seconds to even see his chest rise and fall.

"Are there any more enemies nearby?" I asked the Boards.

"No, Keeper," the Board of the Winds reported. *"Those that did not flee earlier were destroyed by the golems . . . and other forces of nature."*

I peered out and saw that the inner ring of stones was littered with bodies. So much death and destruction, Shadows and Templars alike, and I felt a vague wave of nausea pass through my stomach. I had done this. And if it meant protecting the Boards, I knew in my heart I would do it again. Shalizander was right. What had I become?

"Dismiss the golems," I said to the Board of the Earth.

Its slow, deep voice answered, *"Yes, Keeper."*

I turned back to Simon, and behind me I heard the golems melting back into the ground as the Templars muttered to themselves about dark magics.

"You!" I said to the one who had spoken earlier. "I'll need your assurance."

"I . . . I don't understand," he said.

"I'm going to try and save Simon's life. I cannot be distracted or touched or bothered in any way. You must guard me."

"Such would be Armand's orders anyway," he

said. "Do what you must, but be quick. We need to leave this place."

I knelt next to Simon and felt for his pulse. It was faint and fluttering, and reminded me of my own, faltering heartbeat a few moments ago. He was fading quickly.

"Simon," I whispered. "Don't give up. Don't . . . don't leave me, too."

His eyes were closed, and the lids flickered briefly.

"I . . . I need you, Simon," I said. "We're a team, remember?"

He didn't respond, and I saw that the rags on his wound were soaked through. I was running out of time.

"Shalizander," I said, *"help me!"*

"Simon!" I cried out. "Stay with me, please!"

"All of my gifts are at your disposal, Jenna," Shalizander said.

Her voice was cold, so cold, like the skin on Simon's hand and face. So very cold. *"Do with them what you will."*

I tried to calm myself, and said, *"Where do I begin?"*

I felt her slip into my mind, and opened myself to the invasion. The sensation was not unlike having butterflies in my stomach, except this fluttering was in my head.

"Remove the rags and place your hand over the wound," Shalizander said. *"Let us see what the damage truly is."*

I removed the rags and saw the hole where the bullet had exited his body. It had stopped pumping blood and was now just leaking.

"Quickly," Shalizander said. *"His hourglass empties even as you sit there!"*

Placing my hand on Simon's chest, I did the only thing I knew how to do for certain.

I prayed.

"Father Monk has been mortally wounded in the battle."

"By whom?"

"I do not know, but it was not one of my men. It appears he was shot. An assassin in the dark."

"And the Keeper?"

"She lives. She is praying for him, the battle forgotten."

"A waste, then, of a perfectly good magical weapon."

How long had it been since a truly earnest prayer passed my lips? A month? A year? Five years? I knelt there with my eyes closed, and pieces of the words from one of Father Andrew's prayers, Psalm 102, came back to me in an instant.

"Hear my prayer, O Lord, and let my cry come unto thee.

Hide not thy face from me in the day when I am in trouble . . .

Incline thine ear unto me.

In the day when I call, answer me speedily . . .

My heart is smitten, and withered like grass . . .

Mine enemies reproach me all the day . . .

And they that are made against me are sworn against me . . .

My days have declined like a shadow, and I am withered like grass . . .

But Thou, O Lord, endurest for ever, and thy remembrance unto all generations . . .

O my God, take me not away in the midst of my days, thy years are throughout all generations."

I knew it wasn't all there or completely right, but the words tumbled from my lips. Faster and faster until the only words I could manage were the desperate pleas. "Please, God, please help Simon."

His body grew colder by the second and his heart was faltering. It was . . . it was like a watch with a dying battery, the second hand stopping and starting again. Stopping and starting again.

"Shalizander, hurry! Help him!"

I laid my head down on his chest, listened for his lurching heartbeat. "Simon, come on," I cried. "You have to stay with me."

"Jenna," Shalizander said.

"Help him!" I screamed. He breathed in, out. Stopped. Stopped. Breathed in. Out.

"Jenna," Shalizander repeated. *"He is too far gone. His wounds are beyond me."*

I ignored her. *"Help him, damn it! Don't talk to*

me, just use your so-called powers you keep bragging about."

I felt a hand on my shoulder and shrugged it away. "Leave me alone. I said guard me!"

Armand's voice sounded tired and worn. "Jenna, it's time to . . . to say our goodbyes to Simon. Before he goes."

"I cannot help him, my daughter," Shalizander said. *"There is too much damage. His internal organs are shutting down faster than even I can repair them. His heart—"*

"He has a great heart!" I wailed. *"A great heart and you have to save him!"*

I glanced over my shoulder at Armand. "Help me, for God's sake, help me. He . . . he needs to hold on until we can get help."

Armand's dark, expressive eyes held mine. "He doesn't have that much time, Jenna. Don't waste it in futility. There's nothing more we can do."

"The Templar speaks truly," Shalizander said. *"His wounds are too grievous to be healed by either mundane or magical means."*

"How can that be?"

"The bullet that struck him was magically enhanced. It is likely that it was intended for you. Simon's body is not capable of withstanding the forces at work here."

"It . . . he has to be!"

"He's not," she said. *"I'm surprised he's lasted this long."*

"Jenna," Armand touched my shoulder again.

"Simon was . . . is . . . a man of God. He has been my friend for many years. Please, help me pray for him."

"Whatever comforts you," Shalizander said. *"Death comes for us all in our time."*

"It didn't for you," I said. *"You cheated death."*

Simon took a breath and his chest rose beneath my hand, then fell.

I felt her withdrawing from my mind as she said, *"And when it is my time, no magic in the world will save even me."* Then she was gone.

She'd promised to help Simon, but she had lied. She'd known he was beyond her aid even when she made that promise.

"Please, Jenna," Armand said.

I turned and snarled at him. "Help me save him or shut up."

He knelt down next to me, and reached out to cup my chin in his hands. I saw that his knuckles were cracked and bleeding. His hand shook slightly.

"I have seen death many times, Jenna," he said. "I have looked it in the eye and fought it tooth and claw when to many others it appeared all was lost and doom was upon us. But I know when it has come and when it cannot be fought. Simon's time has come. Here and now. And you must accept that."

I looked around the inner circle of stones. Flickers of fire remained, but the night was rapidly returning. My whole body ached and my mind skittered over thoughts like a flat stone skips on the surface of the water.

"Simon?" I said, shaking his shoulder. "Simon, please . . . please don't go."

Armand began to say something, thought better of it, and stopped.

I leaned down and put my head on his chest.

"Simon, how . . . how come everybody leaves me? You . . . you always had the answers, you know? And I've always got more questions, so you can't leave right now. You have to stay."

In his lungs, I heard the gurgle of blood as he struggled to breathe. His heart was a ragged, irregular movement, barely felt.

"Simon, we've . . . we've got a long ways to go. I . . . *need* you. *Please.*"

"Jenna," Armand said quietly. I heard the teary sound of his voice, but it came to me from so far away. "This . . . this is one of the risks we take. Don't . . . don't make him linger because of your love. Let him go now."

Deep in my chest, I felt the pressure building, like a wall of water pressing against a dam. I lifted Simon's head and cradled it in my arms. There was nothing to be done. He was going to die and I couldn't stop it.

"Simon, *please.*" I heard the words come out as his breathing faltered, faltered . . . and I couldn't stop it. Another death on my behalf, another sacrifice so that I could go on being the Keeper of the Boards.

"NOOOO!" I screamed. I lowered him to the ground, my eyes scanning for the Master Board. If I had the Master Board, perhaps I could still save him. I crawled over a body, shoved another one out of the way.

I couldn't find the strength to stand, but my eyes fell on the Board—my blessing and my curse—and I crawled to it. The air still smelled of burned flesh, of blood spilled and death—so much death—it tasted only of sorrow.

I leaned forward, and grasped the Master Board, Simon's last hope, in my hands.

There was a strange popping sensation in my mind. It was the absence of pressure, like rising to the surface of a deep pool after sitting on the bottom. A wave of relief washed over me as I realized that it was the pressure of keeping the voices of the individual Boards at bay. They were gone, and even Shalizander was silent. I held the Master Board of the Elements in my hands, and it had not consumed me—it had freed me.

My knees cracked as I forced myself to stand. There must still be time to save him, I thought. Still time to figure it out. We'd talked about time and he knew he had to hang on. I stumbled once, and then reached Simon's side, knelt down again.

He was so handsome, his profile outlined in the firelight. Simon was my friend and my mentor and my protector—he was everything to me. He was all I had left.

"Simon," I said, "I've got it. I've got the Master Board. Just hang on a second."

I heard a horrible rattling sound in his lungs and his eyes opened. They were not afraid and he did not seem to be in pain. His hand came up, and he coughed, wincing.

"Jenna," he whispered. "It's . . . okay, you must . . . have . . . a little . . . faith."

"No, it's not," I said. "Just give me a minute. I don't know how . . . what to do yet."

He inhaled, held it, and I felt his fingers brush my cheek.

"Always loved you," he said. "God doesn't mind." His eyes clouded and closed, then opened again, and it was like the first time he'd looked at me. There was that strong spark of connection in his gaze, like we'd known each other forever. Maybe we had. "Be . . . strong, true. There is . . . a mirror of . . . you . . . out there . . ."

The last of his breath left his body and I knew he was gone. His final strength spent on his words.

"I love you, too," I whispered. "I'm so sorry."

I wanted to be strong for him, but the tears came anyway. I couldn't stop them anymore than I could have saved him. I blinked, trying to clear my eyes, trying to hold my sobs inside. My vision sparkled and doubled as I tried to see, tried to find the will to get up and get moving. I knew Armand would want to get out of here.

Overhead, a blazing white light suddenly appeared, the beam resting on Simon's chest. Just like in the hospital in Miller's Crossing and again on the field in Scotland, his body was lined in white and silver light. It poured over him, bathing him in its glow.

I held my breath, wondering what this meant, and then I watched as what I could only assume was Simon's soul rose up out of his body. He stood before me, his spirit whole even if his body was not. He motioned for me to rise and I did, unsure of what to say or think or do. He looked happy, content, and not tired anymore. Where before I had always seen lines of concern around his dark eyes, now there were only peace and calm.

He smiled, and his ghostly hand reached out and caressed my face. I couldn't feel it, but I suspected he could. I blinked back tears, wishing that I could feel his touch one last time.

"I would have gone with you to the ends of the world, my Jenna," Simon's voice said in my mind. *"Or even to the ends of the next world. Do not grieve. All men die in their time, and this was mine."*

"No," I whispered. *"Whatever power He has, tell Him to heal you, to make you whole again. Come back to me."*

Simon chided me gently, *"Who am I to question the Lord? His will shall prevail, and this, too, is part of His plan. I have other work to do."*

"No—you can't go—not now—there's so much left to do—so much I don't know. You can't leave me now. . . ."

"Yes," he said. *"And now you must carry on our quest. You must stop Malkander and gather the rest of the Boards. That is your destiny."*

"Not without you," I said. *"Please, God, not without you."*

He smiled again, and said, *"Yes, without me. That is the way of things."*

"Then I hate it," I said. *"I hate it."*

"I know," he said. *"There is one thing I would tell you before I go."*

"What?" I asked.

"You were right," he said. *"You were right all along."*

"I don't understand," I said.

"I loved you from the moment we met," he said. *"And I always will. Farewell, Jenna."*

"I love you." There was so much more I wanted to say, so many words that hadn't passed between us and never would. Our circumstances had never allowed us to explore a serious relationship and now they never would. For a minute, Simon and I simply looked at one another—he with all the love that he was finally allowed to show me, and me trying to memorize every last detail of his face—and then he smiled one last time and turned away.

He moved toward Armand, and I watched as Armand held perfectly still and made the sign of the Cross. Their eyes locked, and while I don't know what was said between them, I imagined it was the last goodbye between two old friends.

I was crying again as Simon nodded once to Armand, then glanced back at me. Whatever world he was going to wouldn't be mine, and after I had already lost so much, it wasn't at all fair to lose him too. He raised his hand in farewell, flickered briefly, and then, like so many others in my life, he was gone forever.

Clutching the Master Board to my chest, I felt my whole body trembling. So many hurts, so many lives lost to gain this artifact. And there were still another eight more Boards out there, waiting to be found somewhere. How many more would die for me to find them?

"As many as necessary," Shalizander said. *"Death is the inevitable cost of the power we wield."*

I was exhausted, too tired to continue standing, let alone bandy words with Shalizander, and I slumped to the ground. I heard Armand giving orders to his remaining men to prepare for the arrival of the authorities. I couldn't bring myself to care, though some distant part of my mind wondered how he'd be able to explain the massive destruction and the numerous bodies lying throughout Stonehenge. *Let's see you talk your way out of this one.*

Armand called to me, but I ignored him. Even as my thoughts turned again and again to Simon's death, to his ruined body lying on the ground next to me, I knew that one task remained before I could give in to my aching desire to simply close my eyes and rest.

I needed to awaken the Master Board and subdue it to my will. If I failed, everything that had happened before would be without value.

Simon's death would be without value.

"Be wary, daughter," Shalizander said. *"The Master Boards are wholly unlike the individual Boards themselves."*

I was sick of Shalizander, sick of being the Daughter of Destiny.

"Vixisthra," I said. *"Or shut up, if that works better for you."*

She started to say something else, but I cut her off.

"And stop calling me 'daughter.' I hate you for all this. None of this would be happening if it weren't for you and Malkander and your . . . your stupidity."

I heard only silence for a long moment, then Shalizander, her voice icy cold, replied, *"Proceed as you will then, Keeper of the Boards."*

I put the Master Board in my lap and traced my fingers over the tiny runes. I would need better light than I had to study them. Simon would have wanted me to study them, and now, without him to force me to go to libraries, I knew I'd have to do it myself.

Gathering together what was left of my will, I focused on the Master Board, as prepared as I could be, to fulfill my duties as the Keeper of the Elements.

"She has it!"

"The Master Board?"

"Yes! She created it on the central altar and even now seeks to invoke its powers."

"Pull your men back."

"Pull them back?"

"Yes, my dear Cardinal Cepheus. We'll let the Board do our work for us. Send an . . . amenable priest to comfort her later and to pick up the Board. . . . And whatever you do, tell him not to touch it with his bare hands!"

"*I am the Keeper of the Boards,*" I said, sending out the mental call with the tattered remnants of my willpower. *"The Daughter of Destiny and the fulfillment of the prophecy. My will is your will. Our hungers are one. Hear me and obey."*

I felt more than saw Armand kneel down next to me, and his words came from far away. "Jenna, it's time to go now."

"I'm busy," I muttered to Armand. "Leave me alone."

"I am the Keeper of the Boards. My will is your will. Our hungers are one. Hear me and obey!"

"Jenna, the police will be here any minute. We need to get you out of here."

I made a go away gesture with one hand, keeping the other on the Master Board. I strained to hear a response but there was only silence. Had something gone wrong? No, I reasoned. I wasn't calling loud enough, my will wasn't focused enough.

I closed my eyes, shut out the sight of Armand's worried features, the sound of the approaching sirens, the stench of burned flesh and grass until all that I could sense was the void between worlds.

"I am the Keeper of the Boards!" I shouted, trying to focus on the Master Board as hard as I could. *"Hear me and obey!"*

Deep within the silence, I heard a distant sound. I couldn't identify it at first, but it was moving closer. I kept my eyes shut, my focus entirely on connecting to the Master Board. The sound grew slightly louder, and I was reminded of a time my grandfather had taken me to buy honey out in the country. The sound reminded me of the bees, hundreds of them flying from flower to shrub and back to the hive. A low-pitched, humming noise.

"Hear me!" I cried. *"My will is your will. You* must *answer!"*

"Jenna, we're running out of time," Armand called. "We have to go—now!"

The buzzing sound grew louder and more distinct, and I revised my opinion. It wasn't the sound of bees at all, but rather the sound of voices. A hundred voices or a million, the hum of a crowd right before a concert.

I am the Keeper of the Boards, I thought. *And I must complete this task. For Simon.*

Now the sound contained snippets of conversations. I strained to make them out.

"Verily, my lord, the girl must be stopped . . . if we can . . ."

"Energy equals mass times the speed of light squared? Then how do you explain the element of time?"

"Rockslide! Run for your lives!"

"I can hear it, Mama . . . just like you said."

"Who or what is the Keeper of the Boards?"

This last question resonated more loudly, and I chose to answer it. *"I am."*

The voices all began to babble at once, and I resisted the urge to clap my hands to my ears. This was a sound I could not escape. A test I could not afford to fail.

A familiar voice entered the void. *"I am the Board of the Winds. For all these long years, I have been kept by the line, waiting for the last one to hold me. I judge her ready."* The noisy shriek of a gale followed this pronouncement.

Then, *"I am the Board of the Waters. She surpassed an incubus and the test of faith to find me in the City of the Dead. I judge her ready."* An ice storm ripped through the void, and I bit back the urge to shiver.

"I am the Board of the Flames. She overcame an apprentice to the Creator Malkander and the tests of temptation and courage to find me in the heart of Mount Vesuvius. I judge her ready." The void was suddenly lit with fire, walls and sheets of it, a vision of Hell itself.

"I am the Board of the Earth. She successfully opened the portal of worlds and surpassed the test of elemental will to retrieve myself and the key piece in the tomb of Emrys, son of Malkander. I judge her ready." The void shook and wavered, as though an earthquake were possible in a place that didn't exist.

"I am the Keeper of the Boards," I added. *"The last daughter of the Creator Shalizander and the one chosen by destiny to fulfill the prophecy. My will is your will. Hear me, and obey!"*

The void was silent and whatever presence had been making the sounds did not respond. Had I failed some vital test? The Boards had judged me ready.

I tiredly focused my will, prepared to call again, when the Master Board responded.

"I HEAR YOU, KEEPER."

In the real world, I felt the scream torn from my throat before I could stop it. The voice was so massive that I couldn't fathom it, couldn't contain the sound in my pounding head.

"YOU HAVE BEEN JUDGED BY THE BOARDS OF THE ELEMENTS . . ."

I screamed again and opened my eyes. Armand

turned toward the trees and waved at someone and there were lights flashing all around us. Police cars?

"AND DEEMED READY."

I tried to call out for Armand and realized that I was on my knees. My voice was a bare whisper. "Hel—help me," I said.

"FINAL JUDGMENT, HOWEVER, IS RESERVED TO ME."

My head felt like it was going to explode. Each word slammed into my mind like a gigantic fist.

"ARE YOU READY, KEEPER?"

I screamed again, and felt Armand's hand on my shoulder.

"Hang on, Jenna," he said. "Help is coming."

An icy chill passed over me, followed by waves of burning heat. The weight of boulders pressed down on my spine as a wind from some unnamed hell blew hot gale force winds into my face.

Shalizander's voice came to me then, and there was cold laughter behind her taunting words. *"Perhaps you should have listened more closely, apprentice . . ."*

Within the void, I became ancient, then an infant. I wailed and screamed as the Master Board poured its power into me, testing the limits of my strength. I had to push back. If I didn't, it could very well win the contest of wills and all would be lost.

I gritted my teeth and with my mind and my

ruined voice said, *"I . . . am the Keeper . . . of the Boards. Hear me . . . and obey . . ."*

Beyond the trees, in the real world, I saw the phoenix once more, or perhaps just a hallucination of it. It spread its wings and soared into the sky like a rocket, fire trailing behind it.

I wasn't sure what to do, how to control it, so I reached out once again, pulling the tattered fragments of my will around me like a cloak made of newspaper.

"I am . . . the Keeper of . . . the Boards! My will is . . . your will. Hear me . . . and obey!"

The massive voice of the Master Board roared again in my head. *"YOU ARE A FLICKER OF POWER COMPARED TO THE MIGHT OF THE ELEMENTS!"* Another scream was torn from my throat and stars spun in my vision.

Where was Armand? Simon?

What happened to Tom?

How did I get over there? Who am I?

"YOUR WILL IS NOTHING BEFORE MY STRENGTH!"

I wanted to scream then. Wanted to understand. My throat tasted of coppery blood and I could feel it running out of my eardrums. Had I been deafened?

I fell forward onto my face, my outstretched hands still clutching the Master Board that had beaten me so easily. *I should have waited,* I thought, *until I was stronger.*

"SURRENDER!"

My head spun and reason left me. All I could do was curl up into a ball and cry at the pain.

The last of my strength wilted, and I let the blessed darkness take me away into silence.

EPILOGUE

"You must wake up . . ."

"It's time for your medicine, Jenna . . ."

"Look who's come to see you . . ."

The walls are sea-foam green, the floors are white tiles, hard and cold and twelve by twelve. The ceiling is the blue of the Ohio sky an hour after sunrise. The lighting in the room is soft, indirect.

There is no wind here.

No water.

No fire.

No earth.

Time does not exist in this place.

"Daughter, you must gather yourself," Shalizander's voice says.

Who is Shalizander? Why do I know this name?

"I don't know what the cause is, Mr. Anderson. If I did, I'd tell you."

"Will she get better?"

"Only time will tell."

There is no time in this place.

I am separated from the elements and they are separated from me.

"It's time to take your medicine, dear . . ."

"Wake up, now!"

"Come back to me, Jenna . . ."

There is no day, no night. Only the voices and sights of this place.

What is this place? Where am I?

"Don't you want to go home, Jenna?"

"She's been unresponsive for a week now, doctor. Perhaps we should try a more aggressive approach to her therapy?"

"You're her father, so I understand your desire to have her back. We could consider electro-shock therapy, but there are drawbacks to consider . . ."

My father? He is dead.

Everyone is dead. That is why I am here.

This is the afterlife. Heaven. Hell.

"It is a facility for the weak of mind, daughter," Shalizander says. "And that is not you. It is time for you to return to your body."

My body, I think.

My body has breath—the winds. My body has blood—the waters. My body has heat—the flames. My body has carbon—the earth. My body has age—time.

Time. Time is passing, but I do not care how much. I will not let myself care. I will not return to my body. It is elemental and I cannot be connected to the elements.

"Keeper, you are in the void. Now you must come home." This voice belongs to someone else I know. Her name is Malizander. She is dead, too.

Shalizander is supposed to be dead.

Why does she speak to me?

"You have a destiny to fulfill."

What is my destiny?

"You are the Keeper of the Boards."

This phrase sends fear coursing through me. I do not like this phrase. I do not want to be a Keeper of the Boards. I want to be Jenna Solitaire. I miss my grandfather. I want to go home.

"Jenna," a new voice says. I know this voice . . .

This voice brings peace and safety.

"Jenna, I will always be with you, but now you must leave the void and continue your journey."

This is Simon. I love Simon.

Simon is dead.

My wail of grief is all I hear. I do not know how long I cry.

"Be sure to put the tongue guard in, nurse. We don't want her biting it off and swallowing it."

"Of course, doctor."

They are going to shock me. Will this wake me up?

"Only if you let it," Shalizander says.

"It must," Simon says. "There is work you must do."

There is a humming sound, and I am reminded of bees.

"Rolling."

My body stiffens as the electricity pours through me, then begins to convulse. My body is not real. I ignore this sensation.

"Jenna, my girl, it's time for you to come back.

You don't belong in this place. Not yet." My grandfather's voice. A soothing comfort even as the pain ratchets through my muscles.

Why do the dead talk to me? Why did I leave college?

"Jenna, I love you. But it's time. You must wake up."

"I don't want to."

"You must. Time is passing and even now your enemies gather to strike again."

"Without you, there's no reason to go on. I want to stay here. In the dark, in the quiet. Please, Simon. I love you."

"I know, but you must remember yourself. Remember your destiny."

My destiny?

Who am I? I am Shalizander. I am Malizander. I am so many women, young and old, broken on the rack of fate. I am every Keeper and none, because I am different.

"Yes," Simon's voice says. "You are different. You are the last."

"I am Jenna Solitaire."

"Yes. You are Jenna Solitaire. The Keeper of the Boards."

"I must wake up. There's someone here to see me."

"Yes."

"I'm scared."

"Shh . . . I love you. I will be with you. God will be with you. Be at peace."

"Peace."

"Fulfill your destiny. Wake up and be who you are meant to be."

"Yes. I am . . ."

"The Daughter of Destiny," a final voice I know says.

It is the Master Board, and it speaks the truth.

"I was judged."

"Yes, and you were not *found wanting."*

"No?"

"You have done well, Keeper of the Boards. You are fit to serve the purposes of the prophecy."

"I'm scared. I don't want any of this."

"Those who serve the powers of Destiny are rarely afforded a choice and are often scared. Fear not. You have powerful allies in the Boards, strong magic that lies untapped in your veins."

"Magic?"

"You are the Keeper of the Boards. Open your eyes. The Boards have no power over you that you do not give them."

This is truth. A wave of relief washes over me and I am not *afraid. If I open my eyes, I will have to face the world, my destiny, the path laid out for me millennia ago . . . but it is a path I am meant to walk.*

I wake up.

The light is blinding, but I do not fear.

I am the Daughter of Destiny.

I am at peace.

ACKNOWLEDGMENTS

So many people have helped make these first four books in my story possible:

Martin H. Greenberg and Larry Segriff have been invaluable; John Helfers and Susan Chang have provided editorial guidance, tolerated my occasional tantrum, and in the end, made certain that the vision was clear; Kerrie Hughes somehow manages to keep me straight—a job that isn't easy and is generally thankless. Any mistakes you find are undoubtedly mine.

Sherri handled the Starbucks runs and the four "M's" provided emotional support, even when little "R" showed up a bit behind schedule.

Also a special acknowledgment to the music of Kate Bush, Evanescence, and Counting Crows. As much as I travel, thank God for headphones and mp3s!

This is the last one of the first four and without all these people, and so many more, none of this would have been possible.

Thank you all so very much.

ABOUT THE AUTHOR

Jenna Solitaire was raised in Ohio, and now lives the life of a vagabond, searching the world for the next Board. When she was nineteen, she learned that she was the Keeper of the Boards, and her life has been filled with magic and mayhem ever since. Jenna has always believed that sharing her story with others is important and plans on continuing to do so for as long as she can. In addition to this novel, the fourth in the series, her story so far has been chronicled in *Keeper of the Winds, Keeper of the Waters,* and *Keeper of the Flames*.

Please visit her Web site at www.tor.com/jennasolitaire for updates about her adventures and her books, or visit her at http://www.myspace.com/jennasolitaire to read more about her life, or to send her an e-mail. She loves hearing from her readers and she'll try to answer you if she can.

DON'T MISS ANY OF THE BOOKS IN THE DAUGHTER OF DESTINY SERIES

My name is Jenna Solitaire, and everything I thought I knew about myself, my family, and my future is wrong. My life is not my own. It never has been. I just didn't know it—until now. . . .

After the death of her grandfather, nineteen-year-old Jenna Solitaire finds an ancient wooden board hidden away in the attic of his house. Scorched by fire and covered in mysterious symbols, the board fascinates her and scares her at the same time. As does Simon Monk, the handsome stranger who has come into her life, claiming to know about the board. Even more frightening is the voice whispering in Jenna's head, calling her "Keeper." Does Jenna have power over the winds, as Simon claims? Is she truly the Daughter of Destiny?

My name is Jenna Solitaire—and I am the Keeper of the Boards. I have the Board of Air. And every day, I hear the voice of the Board of the Waters calling to me. Somehow, I must find it and master its powers—before some-one else does. . . .

Having mastered the power of the Board of the Winds, Jenna travels to Jerusalem to find the Board of the Waters. She is accompanied by Simon Monk, who seeks the Boards on behalf of the Vatican. Jenna doesn't trust Simon, but he's her only source of information about the Boards. In Jerusalem, Jenna meets Saduj, a local guide who claims to be able to help them find the Board they seek. Simon is suspicious, but Jenna finds herself strangely attracted to Saduj. Jenna must find the Board before it awakens and causes unimaginable destruction. But will she lose her heart—and possibly her life—in the process?

My name is Jenna Solitaire, and I am the Keeper of the Boards. With the elements of Air and Water at my command, I now go in search for the most dangerous Board I have sought so far—the Board of the Flames.

From the searing desert of the Middle East, Jenna and Simon travel to the ancient city of Pompeii, following the clues to the hiding place of the Board of Fire—also known as the Board of the Flames. But Peraud is hot on their trail, and is more determined than ever to claim the two Boards the Keeper already possesses. Jenna must also contend with her growing attraction to Simon, who is torn between his desire for her and his sacred duty to the Church.